The Summer of Falling in Love

LIZ DAVIES

To my mum.

CHAPTER 1

Maths was definitely Theo's "thing", which was a bit of a relief considering he was a maths teacher. He just didn't think he was all that good at it. Teaching, that is – not maths. He was really good at maths. Or he had been when he was younger. Everyone had told him so, and of course he believed them. His exam results confirmed it, as did his degree from Oxford; Oxford Brookes University, not the Oxford University, although he did tend to just say Oxford if anyone asked because it sounded more impressive. He supposed he might have gone on to do great things in the world of mathematics if he'd been so inclined, but instead he'd ended up doing a Post Graduate Certificate in Education and then was offered the first teaching job he'd had an interview for.

He'd taken it.

Perhaps, in hindsight, it hadn't been one of his

better decisions.

Eight years on and he still loved maths – the purity of it, it's empirical nature, the absoluteness of it. You knew where you stood with maths. Maths didn't answer back. Maths didn't balance precariously on two legs of its chair, flicking spit balls at the person in the seat in front of it. Maths didn't slouch, or give sullen glares, or lie about its homework. It didn't call you names, or refuse to behave, or threaten to fetch its rowdy, rather nasty father in to "sort you out". It didn't take drugs or turn up for your lesson drunk, and neither did it throw a chair across the room and storm out of your class in a fit of unwarranted and unpredictable teenage anger.

Yes, maths was good. Teaching? Meh, not so much.

'You look as though you've just had 10.3,' Vicky said when he staggered into the staff room and heaped three spoonfuls of coffee into his mug, followed by an equivalent amount of sugar, and he didn't usually take more than one. Today, though, he needed the extra energy boost.

'How can you tell?' he asked.

'Dazed expression, trembling hands, the urge to end it all written on your face…?' Vicky gave him a sympathetic smile.

Yeah, that just about summed it up. Someone, he forgot who, had once told him that children were the most innocent creatures on the planet. They obviously hadn't met 10.3.

Thirty-one mixed gender fourteen and fifteen-year-olds (thirty-two if you counted Ronnie Elder, who was supposed to be in Theo's class but whom he hardly ever set eyes on), some of them from fairly deprived backgrounds, many of them with some kind of special educational need, and all of them with attitude and a sense of entitlement, were a force to be reckoned with. 10.3 was also the class which received the most amount of attention and resources for the least gain, in his opinion.

The top set, 10.1, could be challenging at times, and the bottom set, 10.5, had its own problems, but 10.3, stuck perfectly in between the most able and the least able classes, was an absolute nightmare.

Every teacher hated them.

It might be wrong and it might go against the grain, but if they were honest every member of staff would say the same. If they were allowed to say it, which they weren't – they could possibly face a disciplinary panel for even thinking it. It wasn't politically correct to admit to disliking one child, let alone a whole classful of them. But the haggard expressions and the defeat lurking in the depths of bloodshot eyes in every staff member after trying to teach them, told its own story.

Theo wrapped his hands around his mug and blew

on his coffee. He only had ten minutes in which to drink it (there was the number ten again; he seemed to be plagued by it today), and if he wasn't careful, he'd be forced to drink it at a temperature more suited to melting lead. He'd lost count of the number of times he'd gulped scalding hot liquid down his poor throat and burnt the roof of his mouth in the process.

'Thank God it's Friday, eh?' That was from Lesley, who taught design technology, and had worked at Robert Crouch High School all her working life. 'And there's only one more week to go and then it's the summer hols. Yay!' She did jazz hands with a big grin on her face.

Theo would have joined in but, as she said, there was still another whole miserable week of term to go. There were a couple of positives about the forthcoming week, though. The Year 11s had already left school having completed all their GCSE exams, so that was one less class to teach next week. As for the rest of the pupils, Years 7 and 8 were on a school trip on the one day, Years 9 and 10 were out on another, no one taught any lessons on the last day, and to be honest, half of the kids wouldn't turn up for the remaining few days anyway. So, it was an easy-ish week. Then he had a whole six weeks of freedom. Bliss. Sheer bliss. He was looking forward to the summer holidays immensely and the knowledge that they were just around the corner had been the only thing keeping him sane during this last half term.

Not that he had any plans, because he didn't. He'd toyed with the idea of going abroad for a week or two, but he didn't want to go on his own. His mum and dad had asked if he'd like to go with them, but honestly, he was thirty years old. Going on hols with your parents was obligatory when you were a kid, and possibly a relief when you had children of your own because there'd be a couple of extra pairs of hands to look after your little darlings. But it wasn't the done thing when you were his age. As for going with his friends, all of them were either married or in long-term relationships, and any holidays they took invariably involved their other halves.

'Going anywhere in the summer?' It was April (politics and law) who'd asked.

'I'm not sure,' he said, as he usually did. 'Are you off anywhere nice?' He knew she was because he'd heard her talking about it the other day, and guessed she'd only asked him about his plans so that she could tell him all about hers.

'Peru, for a whole month,' she squealed and clapped her hands. 'I can't wait!'

'Paddington Bear,' Theo said, for no real reason other than whenever anyone mentioned Peru he thought of the bear.

April gave him a doubtful look. 'Yes. Right. Ha ha. Paddington Bear. Darkest Peru and all that. What about you, Michael?' She turned to one of the English teachers. 'Are you and Charlotte going anywhere?'

Theo let the conversation wash over him as he sipped his coffee, wondering what to do with himself this weekend.

Tonight was takeaway night (Fridays always were) and a film or a box set, but the rest of the weekend stretched in front of him depressingly empty apart from the usual tasks of shopping, laundry, and cleaning. He supposed he could bite the bullet and do a bit of work in the garden. At this time of year, there was always something that needed doing, usually the lawn. It grew like wildfire and he was forever mowing it. He was tempted to dig it up and either gravel it over or stick patio slabs in its place, but if he did that he knew his granny would turn in her grave.

God bless her, she'd loved her garden and his conscience wouldn't let him do that, no matter how fed up he became with incessantly growing grass and bushy bushes that needed to be cut back several times a year.

The last couple of lessons dragged by, with the saving grace of lunch in between to recharge his depleted batteries, until finally 3.30 p.m. arrived, and he was out of the door almost at the same time as the kids, along with every other member of staff in the school, except for the caretaker and the cleaners. Heck, even the head teacher, Mr Fitzpatrick, couldn't wait for a Friday afternoon to arrive, and often planned a meeting which meant he was off-site from about midday onwards. By the end of the week, they'd all had enough and the lure of a bottle of wine or three to drown the sorrows of the previous five days, proved irresistible to most of them.

When he arrived home, Theo gleefully stripped off his works clothes and threw them in the general direction of the laundry basket and got changed into a pair of slouchy jogging bottoms and an old T-shirt. It was too early to eat, but he ordered a takeaway to be delivered in an hour or so, and he whiled away the time between now and then with deciding what he wanted to watch later.

After a great deal of soul searching, the decision was made. He'd watch John Wick. Definitely the first film in the series, and probably the second. After that, he'd have to see whether he could keep his eyes open. He was always knackered on a Friday (although to be fair, he wasn't much livelier on a Saturday or Sunday) and he had a habit of falling asleep in the chair, only to wake up stiff and cramped and have to drag himself off to bed where he'd invariably lie awake for ages and not be able to drop back off.

To give himself a fighting chance of seeing the films

through to the end, he decided to start watching the first one now while he waited for his food to arrive, so he settled back in his favourite armchair and immersed himself in some senseless violence. Actually though – and he'd had this very same conversation with several people – the violence wasn't entirely senseless although it was extremely excessive. If those witless thugs had just left John Wick alone, then none of the ensuing bloodshed would have needed to take place. The men might have got away with nicking his car, but doing what they did to the dog (after watching it the first time, Theo always fast forwarded through that bit because it upset him) was a step too far.

And the fact that the dog had been a present from John Wick's dead wife, sent to John from beyond the grave because she knew she was dying…? Well, it was only to be expected that violence would be forthcoming. Lots of it. There was a lesson to be learned – actions had consequences.

10.3 could certainly do with learning that particular lesson… but when the school's hands were tied in terms of discipline (except for being excluded and most kids saw that as a bonus day or two off school and a badge of honour), there were no real consequences.

Cross with himself for thinking about work on his precious time off, he brought his attention back to the

TV. Pure escapism that's what this film was, and when he was lost in movies like this one, he could imagine himself as the main character doing all those heroic and mostly unbelievable things. It made a nice change from being a maths teacher.

The ring of the doorbell a short while later brought him back to the real world and he paused the film, his mouth already watering at the thought of the Singapore vermicelli rice noodles he'd ordered. But when he opened the door it wasn't the Chirpy Chinese delivery man who was standing on his step; it was his mother.

'Why didn't you use your key?' he asked her, hoping his meal wouldn't be too long and that if it arrived when his mum was still here that she wouldn't want to share it.

'Your dad's in the car,' she told him.

'So?' he peered beyond his rather overgrown hedge and into the lane, seeing a figure in the driver seat of the blue VW Passat. He gave his dad a wave. His dad didn't wave back, and Theo shook his head slightly; his parents were becoming more eccentric by the day.

'I want you to come and look at something,' his mum said, tugging on his sleeve.

Theo wrestled himself free. 'What, right now?'

'Yes, now.'

'Will it take long? I'm expecting my takeaway to arrive any minute.'

'Um, yes and no.'

'Which is it?'

'Come out to the car and I'll show you.' She caught hold of his hand and tugged some more.

'Dad's not gone and got his seatbelt stuck again, has he? Because if he has, he'll need to get the AA out like he did last time.' He dragged his hand out of hers and thought he'd better put some shoes on.

'It's not the seatbelt,' she assured him, and she trotted quickly down the path and was out through the gate before Theo had a chance to stuff his feet into a pair of old trainers which he kept by the front door in case he forgot it was bin collection day and had to dash outside in a hurry. He followed somewhat slower and rather reluctantly.

His mum was standing by the open driver's door and bending down to look inside. It was the damned seat belt; he just knew it. His dad had managed to jam the mechanism once before and had been stuck in it for ages.

But when he got closer, Theo realised his father was sitting half in and half out of the car, and was holding something in his arms. Something furry and wriggly. Something that had put a gooey expression on the faces of both of his parents.

It was a puppy.

'Is this what you want to show me?' he asked. 'A

dog?'

'Isn't she cute?' That was from his dad, who'd never before said the word "cute" in his life, as far as Theo knew.

She was. A little golden blonde bundle of nose and paws, with two brown button eyes and a black button nose.

'Her name is Poppy, she's eleven weeks old and she's a Cockapoo,' his mum told him.

'A what?'

'Cockapoo – a cross between a Cocker spaniel and a poodle.'

'That's nice. What made you decide to get a dog?' Theo heard a car approach and glanced up, hoping it would be his food.

It wasn't. His stomach gurgled loudly, and he let out a sigh of disappointment as one of his neighbours drove past and pulled into their drive.

'Why don't you hold her?' his mother suggested, and his dad thrust the dog at him, leaving Theo no choice but to grab hold of the little creature as gently as he could.

He was rewarded by a warm wet lick on his nose.

'That's not very hygienic,' he stated, trying to wipe off the offending slobber by rubbing his nose on his arm. The dog gave him another lick, this time on his cheek. He pulled a face.

'She likes you,' his mum said. 'Doesn't she, Gerald?'

His dad nodded enthusiastically. 'She does. She didn't give me any doggy kisses.'

Doggy kisses? Were the pair of them going soft in the head? Should he start worrying about early onset dementia? They weren't that old, only in their fifties, but he'd read that it could strike at any time.

His mother was rooting around on the back seat of the car and Theo saw a squishy dog bed piled high with carrier bags. She pulled the whole lot out and plonked it down on the pavement.

Dear God, she wasn't going to insist on showing him everything they'd bought for this pooch, was she?

'Right, Wendy, is that the lot?' his dad asked, and without waiting for an answer he swivelled around in his seat and pulled the door shut.

Theo's mum hurried around to the passenger side and got in.

His dad wound the window down.

'Er, haven't you forgotten something?' Theo asked, holding the puppy up.

'No, I don't think so,' his mum said. 'Have we forgotten anything, Gerald?' She slapped a hand to her forehead. 'Yes, we have – we forgot to tell you that she's had all her injections, but she can't go out for a walk for another seven days. Her paperwork is in one of the bags.'

'Wait, what? I don't understand. What are you talking about, and can you please take your dog with you? I've got a Chinese takeaway coming shortly.'

'It's not our dog, son, it's yours,' Gerald said.

'What?'

'You thought it would liven him up a bit, didn't you Wendy?'

His mum nodded vigorously. 'You're stuck in a rut, Theo, but Poppy will soon get you out of it. You can't sit at home moping about all day when you've got a puppy to look after.'

His dad started the engine and put the car into gear. Theo watched helplessly, the puppy wriggling in his arms.

'I don't mope around all day; I have a job, in case you've forgotten,' he protested, thinking that if this was a joke, it wasn't in very good taste.

'A part time one. It's the times when you're not in school that your mother is talking about.'

Theo's mouth dropped open. Part time indeed! The cheek of it. 'I'll have you know that teaching is a full-time job and—'

'Three months off a year and you're home most days by four o'clock. Your dad doesn't get home until six-thirty, and he has to leave the house in the morning by seven.' His mum folded her arms and stared at him defiantly.

'There's all the lesson preparation and the marking, and we have a staff meeting every Tuesday,' Theo added, desperation beginning to creep in.

'Part time,' Wendy reiterated firmly. 'You do most of that at home with your feet up on the coffee table. Think of your father, working himself into an early grave, and count your lucky stars you're not out of the house for nearly twelve hours a day.'

Theo gritted his teeth, determined not to bite any harder than he had done already. It was pointless arguing with them – as soon as he'd mentioned going into teaching his parents had seen it as the soft option and not the bloody hard work that it really was. No matter what he said, he'd not yet been able to convince them otherwise.

'Don't forget,' his father said, 'the dog isn't to go outside for a week. The garden's OK, the breeder said.'

'But, but…' Theo spluttered. They couldn't seriously be leaving the dog with him. Could they?

They could, he realised, as the car moved slowly off.

His father stuck his head out of the driver's window and hissed at him as he pulled away, probably in the hope that Theo would forgive him, 'Just remember son, I tried to talk her out of it, but you know what she's like when she gets an idea in her head. There's no talking her out of it. Good luck.'

And with that, the car sped up and disappeared around

the bend in the lane, leaving Theo standing on the pavement holding a puppy that he had absolutely no idea what to do with, and most definitely didn't want.

CHAPTER 2

What on earth had they been thinking, Theo wondered? His parents must be losing their marbles. "Liven him up a bit" indeed. He was lively enough already, thank you very much.

And what was he supposed to do with this, he mused, staring down at the dog. It was looking curiously back at him. Talk about being left holding the baby – he had been left holding a puppy he didn't want, didn't have time for, and had next to no idea how to care for.

They'd just have to take it back to wherever it had come from. He couldn't keep it. He didn't *want* to keep it. He had enough on his plate as it was, without being responsible for a dog. And what was he supposed to do with it while he was in work, eh? Had they thought of that? Even he, who had no experience with anything canine, knew it was hardly fair to leave a dog on its own all day.

They must be playing some kind of joke on him. They were probably parked around the corner laughing their socks off. Not that they'd ever played any practical jokes that he knew about, but there was always a first time. And his mum did have an odd sense of humour on occasion.

He stood patiently waiting for them to come back, and as he did so he wondered what had possessed them to get a dog. As his mum just pointed out, his dad worked long hours and his mother still worked more or less full time, although she had been making "I need to retire" and "I'm getting too old for this working nonsense" noises recently. Plus they had active social lives, both separately and as a couple, so how they were going to fit looking after a dog into their daily routine he had absolutely no idea.

When a car he recognised came into view, Theo began to lose patience. His food was here, and this silly joke had gone on long enough. With a dramatic sigh, he strode into the hallway to fetch his wallet, and popped the dog in the kitchen, shutting it inside. Then he went back outside, paid for his meal and gathered up the dog bed and its overflowing contents and marched back indoors. He was tempted to leave it on the pavement to teach them a lesson, but that would mean stooping to their level and he was determined not to do that.

Dumping the lot on the sofa, he reached for his phone. Enough was enough. They'd had their fun and now it was time to take their dog home and leave him to eat his supper in peace.

No answer.

He tried again. Still no answer.

They were acting like a pair of kids. Worse, in fact. The children he taught would have come to their senses ten minutes ago. Playing a joke on him was one thing, but this was ridiculous.

Right. If they were going to carry on playing silly buggers, then he was going to carry on with his evening and ignore them. If they expected him to freak out, then he'd do the exact opposite. They'd have to come back for the dog eventually and when they did, he'd be totally in control. Ha! He'd turn the tables on them, and pretend that he really did think they were serious and insist on keeping the pup when they tried to take it home. That would teach them not to play silly games.

He grabbed the dog's bed and its contents once more and opened the kitchen door.

Before he'd even taken a single step towards the spot where he intended to put the basket, a small body hurled itself at him, whimpering hysterically, it's whole back end wriggling uncontrollably and the tail whipping from side to side as if the little creature was trying to become airborne.

He dropped to his knees and drew it to him. The poor thing must be traumatised. It had probably only been taken from its mum and littermates earlier today, and then it had been carted around in his parents' car undoubtedly thinking that they were its new family, only to be shoved into his arms and abandoned by them. Then he'd gone and shut it in a strange room (even if had been for less than five minutes) all by itself. No wonder it was weeing all over the floor.

And the legs of his joggers.

Great. He'd tell his mum she'd have to disinfect his floor before she took the dog home with her. It was only fair. Her dog, her mess, her responsibility.

Gingerly he picked the puppy up, mindful of its wet paws where it had stepped in its own pee, and reached for a roll of kitchen towel. After he'd mopped up the mess and wiped its paws, he took it upstairs with him while he changed into a clean pair of jogging bottoms, unwilling to leave it on its own again in case of any further accidents. Wee he could cope with (just), it was poop he wasn't so keen on.

Wearing fresh joggers and back in the kitchen, Theo placed the pup down on the floor and proceeded to unpack the dog bed and the rest of the stuff his parents had left. When he finished, he glanced at the clock and saw that fifteen minutes had gone by since they'd driven off. Surely they must be back soon? Just how long were they going to string this out for?

He placed the bed underneath the kitchen table so it was out of the way, and put the food and water bowls by the side of the fridge. Then he rooted around in the bags to see what else was in them. Collar and lead in pink with diamantes on them (his mother's choice, he guessed). A small soft-bristled brush. Wet wipes and an antiseptic spray. A large pack of something called puppy training pads. A selection of toys, including a ball, a length of brightly coloured twisted rope, and some cuddly stuffed animals. Finally, several packets of puppy food (lamb in rich gravy, chicken with rice and vegetables – crikey, this dog would eat better than him) and some chews and treats completed the haul. They'd thought of everything.

It was about time they thought about fetching their dog. His food was getting cold and he wasn't sure how much longer he could keep up the pretence of being delighted to have been given a puppy.

His stomach grumbling, he retrieved the takeaway from the living room and dished it onto a plate. He was starving and he wasn't prepared to wait any longer. If his daft parents turned up now, then they could jolly well sort the dog out themselves.

The puppy plonked its fluffy little bottom down on the kitchen floor and watched his every move. As he warmed his Chinese up in the microwave and got some cutlery out of the drawer, he was conscious of its black button eyes fixed firmly on him. Its intense and unwavering stare made him feel slightly uncomfortable. Its expression (if dogs could be said to have an expression) was solemn and rather worried. If he was being honest, the poor little thing looked rather frightened.

'I won't hurt you, little one,' he said to it in a soothing tone, and was rewarded with a cock of its head.

Then the microwave pinging made it jump and sent it scurrying backwards a few steps, undoing all his good work.

'It's just the microwave,' he told it, then asked himself why he was explaining microwave noises to a dog.

Its tail was between its legs, its back slightly hunched, and it looked more frightened than ever, but its nose was twitching at the smell of his Singapore vermicelli rice noodles and he wondered if it was hungry. If it was, it could jolly well wait until he'd eaten his own meal – if, that is, his annoying mother and father hadn't returned before then, and if they had, then they could feed it at their own house instead of his.

Taking his food into the living room, he settled

down in his armchair with a tray balanced on his knees, and picked up his fork. The implement was heavily laden and halfway to his mouth when he became aware he was being watched.

He'd left the kitchen door open, and the puppy had crept into the living room and was peering around the edge of the door, studying him.

Theo pressed "play" on the remote and resumed watching the film.

The dog continued to stare at him.

He glanced at it out of the corner of his eye.

It hadn't moved.

He ate another mouthful.

Its nose twitched again, and it licked its lips.

Damn and blast! It was making him feel guilty now. Maybe if he gave it one of those sachets, it would stop staring at him. How was a bloke supposed to eat when he was being stared at like a monkey in a zoo?

With a sigh, he paused the film once more, then got up and put his tray down on the seat of his chair. 'Come on,' he said. 'Are you hungry? Do you want something to eat?'

The dog cocked its head again, backing away when he walked towards it.

'You are a funny little thing, aren't you? I'm not going to hurt you,' he told it for the second time. 'Look, I've got food.' He waved a sachet at it.

The puppy blinked with one eye and stared solemnly at him.

He bent down to pick up its bowl, opened the sachet and squeezed the contents out, wrinkling his nose at the smell. 'Yummy,' he said as he broke the gelatinous lumpy mass apart with a fork. Was the whole sachet too much? Not enough? How much did you feed a dog anyway? It clearly depended on their size, larger dogs needing more fuel than smaller ones (basic maths, there), but did it depend on their age too? Did puppies need more food than adult dogs of the same size? Or less?

Oh, what the hell! It didn't matter – his ridiculous parents could sort that out in time for its next meal. It wasn't his problem. He popped the bowl on the floor and turned around, expecting to see the dog waiting anxiously.

The puppy wasn't in the kitchen.

When he stuck his head around the door and peered into the living room, he found it up on its back legs with its nose on his plate, chewing happily, its tail wagging furiously.

Before he could say a word, it had wolfed down another mouthful.

'Oi! That's mine!' he yelled.

The little dog immediately dropped to the floor, its tail curled under its body, and whimpered. When he approached to rescue his plate, it slunk away.

Wonderful. Now he'd managed to frighten a small puppy. This evening was going from bad to worse.

Wrinkling his nose at his takeaway, he picked up the tray and removed it to the kitchen. He'd throw the food out later, after he'd convinced the dog that he wasn't as bad as it thought he was. He dumped his dinner on the countertop and returned to the living room.

The dog was shivering behind a chair.

'I'm sorry,' he crooned, kneeling down next to it. 'I didn't mean to scare you, but that was my supper you were eating and I'm not sure human food is good for a dog.'

The pup stared at him with wide eyes and continued to cower.

Theo thought for a moment; he was quite a large fella, six-foot-two and with broad shoulders. The dog didn't know him from Adam, he'd just yelled at it, and was now looming over it like the wrath of God. So, if he looked at it from the pup's point of view, no wonder it was terrified.

He decided to try a different tack and give it some space. If he sat quietly in the chair and it saw that he was no threat, it might come out from its hiding place. Besides, he wanted to call his parents again.

He sank into the seat, careful not to make any

sudden moves, and picked up his phone, noticing a WhatsApp message in the *Don't Tell the Missus* group chat. Technically, he supposed he shouldn't be in it considering he didn't have a missus to hide anything from, but the group of lads had all been friends since uni and one of the others was single too (married and divorced, when Theo hadn't even got to the married part yet), so technically the others didn't have a leg to stand on if he wanted to be in the group.

In-laws visiting tonight. Sadie is cooking. I'm trying to pretend it's not happening. What's everyone else up to?

Theo smiled. Mother-in-law jokes were rife with this lot, and Dave didn't seem all that enamoured of his.

Dog-sitting, Theo replied. *Parents gone mad or having a second mid-life crisis.*

The first one had occurred when they'd both got matching tattoos and had bought motorbikes. Except the machines were more on the Vespa end of the biking spectrum, and neither of his parents was comfortable doing more than twenty-five miles an hour on them. To be fair, he wasn't entirely sure the little bikes could actually *go* any faster. They had matching helmets too, round, like marbles perched on their heads. His dad's was blue and his mum's was pink. Cute – *not*. He'd like to see them trying to take a dog out on one of those. Maybe they could get a basket on the front…?

Wish we had a dog. Christine won't let me. She likes cats. Archie had joined in the conversation. He'd been living with his girlfriend for years and had returned to Derbyshire as soon as he'd completed his degree, so most of the contact with him was electronic in nature.

Theo risked a quick glance at the dog. It was sitting on its haunches, still keeping the bulk of the chair between it and him, but at least it didn't look as nervous.

Fancy doing something tomorrow? That was Jenson. **Bella is going shopping with her mum. Baby stuff. How about a pint in town?**

Henry: **Can't. Plans.**

Dave: **I'd love to mate, but we're off to a wedding.**

Henry: **Whose?**

Dave: **Some friend of Sadie's.**

Theo: **I can make it. Where do you want to meet and when?**

Jenson: **The Cardinal's Trumpet at 3?**

Theo: **Great. See you there.**

He had another go at calling his parents. There was still no answer, and he frowned. He was starting to get seriously annoyed now. And he was hungry, although he bet the bloody dog wasn't.

Theo: *The sodding dog ate my Chinese. I shouted at it and now it won't come out from behind the chair,* he typed into the group chat and received a load of laughing face emojis in reply.

Archie: *What sort of dog is it?*

Theo: *I dunno. Cock and poo, I think my mum said. I wasn't paying much attention.*

More laughing emojis, one slap-head Giff and an *Aw man, you crack me up,* swiftly followed.

Archie: *Cockapoo. Cross between a Cocker spaniel and a poodle.*

Dave: *What Archie said.*

Theo: *Bugger off, you lot. I don't care what it is, it ate my dinner.*

Jenson: *Lol. Why are you dog-sitting? Can't imagine you with a dog. Surprised they trust you with it.*

Theo: *Very funny. They rocked up about an hour ago and dumped the bloody thing on me. Said it was mine. I told you they were getting weird.*

Archie: *Yours? So you're not dog-sitting then? You're dog-owning.*

Theo: *They're playing some kind of stupid joke.*

Dave: *Are you sure about that?*

Theo wasn't, not at all, but that's what he was trying

to make himself believe. But as time was going on and there was neither sight nor sound of his parents, he was beginning to think they weren't coming back for it.

Then he noticed a text from his mother. ***Poppy is yours. Deal with it. And stop calling us. We're going swinging.***

Eh??? Theo sat up straight in shock. They're doing *what?*

#Singing. Stupid autocorrect. The second text followed hard on the heels of the first and he blew out his cheeks in exasperation.

It wasn't the idea that his parents might be swingers that bothered him; well, it *was*, but he had bigger fish to fry and he really, really didn't want to think about them having a "private" life. Yuck. Just yuck. It was the realisation that they'd meant what they'd said about the dog.

It was his.

He was now the not-so-proud, very reluctant and totally clueless owner of a dog.

Just what the hell was he supposed to do with it?

CHAPTER 3

Okaaay, he knew he couldn't take care of it in the long-term (he worked full-time for goodness' sake!) but he could manage a few days until he found someone to take it off his hands. It – *she* – was undeniably cute. Even his gruff dad had admitted as much (wait until the next time he saw his father – he'd give him a piece of his mind), so it should be easy to find it – *her* – a suitable home.

With a heavy sigh, he rang his mother again, not expecting any response, but to his surprise she answered.

'Finally! I've been calling you for hours,' he exclaimed.

'Don't exaggerate. What do you want? I told you we're going singing.'

'What time will you be back?'

About three o'clock next Friday.'

'Eh?'

'Next Friday, at three in the afternoon,' she repeated slowly and deliberately, enunciating every word clearly as if English wasn't his first language (it was his only language, but that was by the by).

'I heard you the first time,' he said through gritted teeth. 'Where are you exactly?'

'On our way to Harrogate. As for exactly where we are right now, you'll have to ask your father. On a motorway, the M5, I think. Gerald, Theo wants to know which motorway we're on. I said the M5. Am I right?'

Theo heard his dad muttering in the background.

'I'm right.' His mum sounded delighted. 'It is the M5.'

Theo screwed his eyes shut, praying he'd wake any minute now to discover this was all a bizarre dream. 'I couldn't care less what motorway you're on,' he growled. 'Why are you going to Harrogate?'

'I told you why. Heaven help me, but you don't listen to a word I say. We're going singing. With the choir.'

'You aren't in a choir.'

'We are, too!'

'Since when?'

'Last week. Your dad was chatting to a bloke down at the bowls club, who said they're short of members.

He also said they were having their yearly jaunt to Harrogate and there were spaces left on the coach, so we decided to join. We've never been to Harrogate.'

If Theo rolled his eyes anymore, his eyeballs would be in danger of disappearing around the back of his head. 'Do you realise the problems you've caused?'

'Oh, it's not a problem' she assured him cheerily. 'They were glad to have a couple more people on the coach.'

He knew she was being deliberately obtuse. 'Not for *them*, for *me*! What am I supposed to do with a dog when I'm in work all day?'

'I have every faith in you. We both do. You'll work something out. I can pop in lunchtimes to see to the pup when you're back in work.'

'I'm in school *next week*,' he pointed out. 'You'll be in *Harrogate*.' The way he said it, made Harrogate sound like a foreign country, and it might as well be, because his parents were stuck there until the coach brought them back home, and who was going to see to the animal if they weren't around? No one, that's who.

'Are you? I thought the schools broke up today.' She didn't sound at all concerned that by dumping a tiny puppy on him and waltzing off to Yorkshire she was going to make his life extremely difficult next week.

'No, we finish *next* Friday,' he grumbled. 'What am

31

I supposed to do with the dog?'

'You'll think of something,' she repeated. 'It's only for a week, then you've got a whole six weeks to train her.'

'You're going to Harrogate on purpose, aren't you?'

She laughed down the phone. 'We've hardly been kidnapped. We did plan to go on this trip, you know.'

'Was that before or after you came up with the ridiculous idea that I need a dog in my life?'

'You're being very cynical.'

'Me? I wonder why? What is that noise?'

'Singing. I told you, we're in a choir. I've got to go; I can't hear you terribly well and they want your father and me to join in. La, lala, laaaalala—'

Theo hung up. The blighters had planned this down to the finest detail, he realised, making it impossible for him to return the favour of turning up on their doorstep with the dog in his arms, and forcing them to take it back.

And if the pair of muppets who called themselves his parents were on a coach heading for Yorkshire, then he supposed he'd have to try to make his peace with the pup tonight. He didn't like the thought of the dog being scared of him, and she must be terrified enough already without him making it worse.

Theo slid off his chair and onto the floor, and stretched out a hand.

The dog didn't move.

He made clicking noises with his tongue.

The dog still didn't move.

'Poppy, Poppy, come here, girl.' That was her name, wasn't it? He checked his phone to make sure he'd got her name right. 'Come on, Poppy.'

She continued to view him with a wary expression.

How long was he supposed to sit there and wait for her to come out from behind the chair, he wondered, guessing that her patience might outweigh his by quite a considerable amount. Making a decision, he crawled slowly over to her, trying to keep as low to the ground as possible so as not to alarm her any more than he already had, and went in for a grab and scoop manoeuvre.

Before the pup knew what was happening, Theo had lunged forward, scooped her up and was cradling her in his arms. The dog looked up at him and Theo looked down at her. For a moment the pair of them gazed into each other's eyes and Theo felt a little tug on his heartstrings. She was so tiny, so fragile, and so very timid. Underneath her fluff-ball fur, she was little more than skin and bones, and his instinctive reaction was to cuddle and comfort her. She was also very cute. If you like that kind of thing.

They sat there for a while, Theo wondering what he should do now. He had no idea what the dog might be thinking, but when she began to wriggle and squirm, he put her back on the floor.

Poppy immediately squatted down and peed.

Yuck. Gross. 'That's nasty,' he said to her, and the pup gave the tiniest wags of her tail and looked at him with a solemn expression.

Wasn't she housetrained yet? Or had the trauma of being taken from the only place she'd ever known and dumped on him, made her forget herself and have an accident? Dear God…

With a sigh, he heaved himself to his feet and went in search of the kitchen roll, wet wipes and that antibacterial spray. As he mopped and cleaned the rug, Poppy continued to watch his every move.

She was a timid little thing, uncertain and wary, and although he felt he should tell her off for peeing in the house, he couldn't bring himself to. Instead, he finished dealing with the mess (not that there was much of it because she was so little), and sat back down on the floor, avoiding the wet patch.

The dog, seeing that he wasn't about to move anytime soon, sat on her own haunches, regarding him with a serious expression.

Theo ignored her. Not because he didn't want any contact, but he thought it best to let her come to him in her own time. With that in mind, he took the film off pause and tried to carry on watching it.

Was he supposed to leave her in the kitchen tonight, unsupervised? If he did, would she chew anything? Should he take her into the garden in a minute, or wouldn't she need another pee for a couple of hours? How big was a puppy's bladder, anyway?

These questions and loads more popped into his head and out again in rapid succession, until eventually he reached for his phone and searched for some answers, the film playing in the background, totally ignored.

Crikey, there was an awful lot of information out there, some of it conflicting, but he did discover that puppies had tiny bladders (he suspected as much), needed to eat two or three small meals a day (none of them consisting of a Chinese takeaway), that he should take her outside for a pee every half hour or so, and that poops were more likely to occur after a meal.

Theo froze.

Where was the dog?

He glanced from side to side, his eyes darting around the room.

The pup was nowhere in sight.

He sniffed. It might be his imagination, but he was sure there was an unpleasant aroma in the air, faint at first but growing rapidly stronger. It smelt suspiciously like poop.

He found her behind the sofa, sitting next to a

noxious pile, still giving him her solemn stare. But he could have sworn there was a glint of mischief in her eyes, and he narrowed his own at her.

Once again he was tempted to scold her, but the stuff he'd read online suggested otherwise, that she wouldn't associate the telling off with the poo unless he caught her in the act. Retrospective reprimands wouldn't work, and would damage any relationship he was trying to build with her. Thankfully she'd done it on the polished floorboards, so it was easy enough to clean up, and he was grateful that she hadn't done it on the rug or else he'd be going out to buy a new one first thing in the morning.

For the second time he cleaned up her mess without comment, but when he was finished (God, that seriously hadn't been pleasant), he picked her up and plonked her down on his lap, this time in the chair. He was sick of sitting on the floor when he had a perfectly good three-piece suite to slouch on. He'd read on one of the sites that he should start as he meant to go on and that he needed to decide right from the beginning what boundaries to set (like not having the dog on the sofa), but considering he had no intention of keeping her, he didn't care about setting boundaries. All he cared about was not having a numb backside and stiff knees from sitting cross-legged on the floor. Let her new owners deal with any bad habits she may pick up during the short amount of time she lived in his house. Besides, for all he knew, they might be quite happy with her clambering all over the furniture.

Not that she was clambering. She wasn't even moving, and Theo stared at her in concern. Was she OK? He leaned closer. The slight rise and fall of her chest sent a wave of relief flooding through him. Sleeping, that's what she was doing. Thank God for that. For one awful second, he'd thought something terrible had happened. He might not want to keep her, but he certainly didn't want anything to happen to her.

He'd have to make sure she went to a good home, he thought, ruling out a rescue centre. If he took her to the Dogs Trust or the RSPCA, he'd have no control over who adopted her. He was sure both organisations wouldn't have any trouble rehoming her (look how cute she was) and would do all the necessary checks, but he wanted to see for himself who her new owners would be. He had a feeling this little pup would need a great deal of love and reassurance. She reminded him of a girl in Year 7 with her quiet nature and the worried depths in her eyes. Channi, that was the child's name. She was small for her age and delicate, and had the look of a scared puppy about her. The same look that had been on Poppy's face. Apparently, Social Services were involved and there was talk of putting her into care. Theo prayed Channi would be placed with a family who could give her the love that he suspected she sorely lacked.

Which was why he'd have to be the one to find the dog a good home, and not trust it to a faceless organisation, no matter how caring they were. He wanted to check out her new family for himself, and if he wasn't happy with them, then he'd simply have to look for another.

'Thanks, Mum,' he muttered. It was all her fault he was in this position. He was under no illusion that his mother had been the driving force behind it. His dad would never have thought up anything so ridiculous, let alone have gone through with it. Theo wasn't surprised that his dad hadn't been able to prevent it, though. Once his mum got an idea in her head it would take an army to get her to change her mind. Which was why he knew he didn't stand a cat in hell's chance of getting his mother to accept that she was wrong and take the dog back to where it came from.

Were you able to get refunds on animals anyway? Was there such a thing? And did the Consumer Rights Act cover dogs? He suspected it didn't.

Poppy stirred and he glanced down at her anxiously.

His heart melted when he realised her paws were twitching and she was making little sucking noises in her sleep. Aw, bless. She really was quite adorable – when she wasn't soiling his floor or eating his tea.

Apricot-coloured fluff covered her from nose to tail, with slightly darker patches on the ends of her ears, and when he gently ran his fingers through her wavy coat, he saw that underneath the top layer the fur beneath was a pale cream. As far as dogs went, this one was very pretty indeed. And now that she'd finally relaxed enough to fall asleep, he discovered that cuddling a snoozing puppy was quite a pleasant thing to do.

He felt his own eyelids drooping and although it wasn't even dark outside yet, he thought he might have a little nap of his own. It had been manic in work this week, what with the end of year exams for most of the school and having to do all the associated marking. In fact, he should be doing some now. His Year 9 test papers wouldn't mark themselves, and neither would the Year 7's homework. He wasn't watching the film (John Wick was still busy killing people at the rate of one every ten seconds or so) so he may as well make use of the time. The marking had to be done whether he did it now or in a last-minute rush on Sunday night – which is what usually happened.

But it was so nice sitting here, the dog's hot little body resting in his lap (he worried that she had a fever because she was so warm, but after he'd checked online and discovered that a dog's temperature was higher than a human's, his concern faded) that he decided not to disturb her for a while…

He was woken up by a cold wet nose on his neck and warm puppy breath on his skin.

Theo found himself giggling.

It tickled. Her snuffles, followed by a couple of swift flicks of her tongue, had him laughing like a loon.

'Stop it,' he cried, making no move to push her away.

Poppy wriggled up his chest, her paws scrabbling on his T-shirt as she tried to climb higher up his body and reach his face.

He turned his head away and was rewarded by a wet nose in his ear. 'Geddoff,' he giggled, hunching his shoulder and screwing up his face.

Her tail was wagging furiously, and she was plainly enjoying herself.

'Ow!' Crikey her teeth were sharp. He rubbed his ear where she'd nipped him, and she nibbled at his fingers. 'You can't be hungry,' he said. 'Not after all that Chinese food.'

But then again, he was often hungry himself after he'd eaten the same thing, so maybe she was.

After carrying her out to the kitchen, he put her down by her bowls. Poppy stood there for a minute, uncertainly, her tail down, and he guessed that this might be her standard reaction to anything new. She'd been in the kitchen earlier, but having been in the living room for a couple of hours, she might be feeling nervous all over again.

Maybe she needed a wee?

His eyes went to the door leading out to the garden, and he briefly debated whether to take her outside, but thought better of it. Best to get her used to the house and him, before he tried to persuade her that the garden would be a good place to relieve herself.

'Do you want to go potty?' he asked her.

Poppy gave him one of her inscrutable looks.

'Potty? Wee-wee? Poo?' He knew she had absolutely no idea what he was saying, but he couldn't help himself. Talking to the dog seemed a totally natural thing to do and using a slightly babyish tone was part of it. He was just thankful that no one could hear him, otherwise he'd never live it down.

Then he remembered the large pack of puppy pads and he had a light-bulb moment. Opening the packet, he unfolded a couple and spread them on the floor around her bed and near the door. With any luck she'd prefer to go on those than on the cold tiles, but the only way to find out for sure was to loiter in the kitchen until she was ready to widdle. Or worse.

It was option number two, in both senses of the phrase, he discovered, after a ten-minute wait watching her slink around the room and stick her nose into every corner, cautious and uncertain. When the slinking became more of a pacing and she began to twirl around in circles, he realised that this was her "tell" after she deposited a little present slap bang in the middle of one of those pads.

'Good girl!' he cried, as she looked at him uncertainly. 'There's a clever girl.'

With a wag of her tail, she trotted over to him, and he ruffled her fluffy ears. If she was going to stay with him for a couple of days until he could sort out a new home for her, then it was probably a good idea that he started the housetraining thing because he didn't want to have little messes all over the place.

She stood on her hind legs, wrapped her chunky front paws around his arm and licked his hand, making soft little whimpering noises in her throat as she did so. He had to admit that she was the epitome of cute, and his heart began to melt.

It took a sleepless night listening to a never-ending succession of puppy howls, barking and yipping, for it to harden once more.

The dog simply had to go.

CHAPTER 4

There was something rather odd and vaguely comforting about having another person in the house. Not that Poppy was a person as such, but she was another living breathing creature sharing his home (albeit temporarily), and it was weird to have to think about anyone other than himself. Her weight on his feet as he sat at the kitchen table marking Year 9's mostly pathetic attempts at their end-of-year tests, was quite pleasant.

However, last night hadn't been as pleasant, and he was sorely tempted to prod the sleeping puppy awake and see how she liked a dose of sleep deprivation. She'd finally quietened down at around four a.m., but the peace hadn't lasted long, because the little sod had woken him again at seven. He couldn't remember the last time he'd seen seven o'clock in the morning on a Saturday, and he hadn't appreciated it. There was little to no chance of persuading her to settle down in her basket and go back to sleep, so he'd got up, cleaned up her accidents, and made them both some breakfast.

He'd taken the dog upstairs with him while he had a shower, not wanting to shut her in the kitchen again and listen to her pathetic and heartrending cries, and she'd sat on the bathmat while he'd showered, then as soon as he'd stepped out of the cubicle she'd had him in fits of laughter as she'd tried to dry his ankles with her tongue.

She'd sat on the bed while he'd got dressed, watching him intently, then followed him down the stairs, her nose touching his leg just to let him know she was there. Or maybe it was for reassurance; he couldn't tell. It was a bit disconcerting to have her constantly watching him, but when he'd plonked himself wearily down on a chair and brought the test papers out of his bag, she must have realised he wasn't going anywhere, because she settled herself down at his feet and promptly fell asleep.

Theo wished he could do the same, but if he gave in and had a nap now, he'd still have the damned marking to do at some point. He was here now, so he might as well get on with it. He didn't want to have school work hanging over his head for the rest of the weekend, and he had an awful feeling that if the pup didn't sleep much tonight either, he'd be in an even worse state tomorrow.

Finally finished, he put the test papers back in his bag and stretched to ease out the kinks in his back. One foot had gone to sleep from being in the same position for too long, and he tried to move it gently so as not to wake the dog, but the instant he shifted position she was awake.

A little nose peeped from beneath the table, followed by a pair of eyes and the rest of her head as she put her paws on the edge of his chair and tried to scramble up onto his lap.

'Do you want to be picked up?' he asked her. 'Would you like a cuddle?'

She dropped back down to the floor and as Theo began to get to his feet, he felt a warm wetness seep through the soles of his stocking feet. Ah. That's what she'd wanted.

Lovely.

With a resigned sigh (he seemed to be doing an awful lot of those recently), he went to fetch the cleaning materials yet again and to change his soggy socks, the puppy following closely behind him.

Note to self, he thought; place the pup on one of her super-absorbent training pads the second she wakes up. It was common sense in a way – a small bladder equalled frequent wees, and she was too young to hold it for long. Like a small child, when she had to

45

go, she had to go.

He scooped her up and she snuggled into him as he held her with one arm, her paws dangling, and he gave her a cuddle, smelling the sweet puppy scent of her and feeling her warm little body close to his.

'What am I going to do with you?' he murmured, his nose buried in the fluff on the top of her head. He hadn't stopped worrying about her all last night – and the problem of how he was going to manage next week loomed larger and larger with every passing hour.

Maybe if he asked nicely, he could take her into school? But, with a grimace, he immediately discounted the idea. There was no way the head teacher was going to allow him to bring a dog into school. It would be too distracting for the kids, and besides, there were other members of staff with dogs who, once Theo had opened the floodgates, would insist they should be allowed to bring their pets to school, too. Then there was probably the insurance issue, and some of the children may be allergic, others may be terrified of dogs… there were probably loads more reasons why he couldn't take Poppy to work, but that was just a few off the top of his head.

He'd better make some other arrangements, he decided, because the only other alternative was to leave her on her own all day and he didn't feel at all comfortable with that option. It wasn't fair on her for a start, and he'd be doing nothing but worrying about her.

He paused. He'd be *worried* about her? Why should he worry——? Oh, yes, because she might destroy his kitchen, that's why. Phew, for a minute there he thought he was starting to get attached to her. And that simply wouldn't do. He had no room in his life for a dog, and no desire to make room for one. Maybe a few years down the line, when he was married and had a kid or two, then he'd think about it. But not right now. He was too busy, what with work and his social life.

He went to fetch his laptop; the sooner he started looking for a solution to the Monday morning problem of what to do with the puppy, the better.

Concentrating on the screen, with the pup sitting on his lap, he had no real idea what he was looking for, but his eyes lit up when he spotted a website advertising doggy day care. You could leave your pooch there all day, dropping the animal off in the morning and picking it up in the evening. For an additional fee they'd collect—— *How much?*

Ouch.

With few obvious alternatives, he gave them a call. It would only be for a week. After that, he should have managed to rehome her, and if not then at least he was off work for a good long time.

'We do have a vacancy for Monday but we need to

assess your dog first to check his or her suitability. We have a space at two-thirty today if you'd like to come along?' The voice on the other end was female and sounded rather bored and nasally.

'Righto, that's great.' It wasn't, because he was supposed to be meeting Jenson for a pint at three, but it would have to do.

'I just need to ask a few questions, if that's OK?' the voice continued.

'Fire away,' he said cheerfully.

'Male or female?'

'Er, male obviously.' Did he honestly sound like a woman?

'Age?'

'Thirty.'

A weird snort carried over the airwaves. 'I meant the dog's age.'

'Ah, I see. And I expect you were asking the dog's gender, not mine. She's a girl.'

'OK. How old?'

'Eleven weeks.'

'I'm sorry, did you say eleven weeks?'

'That's right.'

'Oh, we don't take them that young. They've got to be four months or over, and they must have had their final vaccination two weeks prior to their first session.' She sounded as though she was reading from a script, and the lack of inflection in her voice grated on his nerves. She sounded as though she couldn't care less.

'Can you make an exception?' he pleaded. 'Just this once?'

'No, sorry. It's for your dog's benefit, as well as ours.'

That's that then, he thought as he ended the call. Back to the drawing board. He squinted at the screen again as he clicked on another link. Maybe this would do? The site was called *The Next Best Thing*, as in, the people who cared for your pet when you were unable to, were the next best thing to you as far as your fur baby was concerned, he read (*fur* baby?). They claimed to have a database of dog walkers and dog sitters who would do anything from pop into your house to give your dog a cuddle, right through to looking after your pet in their homes for a couple of weeks while you jetted off to Majorca.

This could be just the thing he was looking for. He registered his details and the pup's, and debated what service he needed. Dog walking wasn't an option for the coming week because she wasn't allowed out yet, so he supposed he'd have to have someone pop into his house to give her a cuddle and some attention. Would once a day be enough, or should he make it twice? There was another option, and that was for him to take Poppy to the dog sitter/walker person before

49

he left for work then fetch her after he finished work.

To be honest, he wasn't entirely comfortable with either scenario. The first one involved giving a complete stranger a key to his house and allowing him or her access to his home. The second meant that Poppy wouldn't know which house she was supposed to be living in or who was her owner, and considering he was going to find another home for her (that was his next task after he'd sorted out her immediate care for the forthcoming week), he didn't want the poor little thing to be even more confused and unsettled than she already was.

He made his decision; the lesser of two evils was to have someone come to the house, so he completed the registration form and sat back; all he could do now was to wait to be contacted by anyone who was interested in the job.

Then he moved on to Gumtree.

A photo or two would help, he soon realised, after scrolling through the site. And he should settle on a price. He was tempted to say that she would be free to a good home, but he thought it might attract the wrong sort of owner. At least if he sold her and not gave her away, he'd know that the family who bought her was serious about wanting a dog.

He was just about to wake the sleeping pup to take a picture or three of her, when he noticed he had a message from *The Next Best Thing*. It was from a woman called Josie Wilde, and there was a photo of her with what he assumed to be her own dog. She looked nice enough. More than nice; she was extremely pretty. Her smile was wide and open – she was almost laughing into the camera as her dog licked her face – and her eyes crinkled slightly at the corners. She had high cheekbones and clear skin, and he found he had enlarged her image and was staring at it quite intently.

Hastily he returned it to its original thumbnail size, and examined her professional details instead. According to the website, she lived 0.7 of a mile from him, had a very friendly Springer spaniel called Crumble, had a Level 2 Animal Care Certificate with Special Pet Dog Care Diploma, a DBS certificate, and had worked with animals all her life. Looking at her, that probably wasn't all that long – she couldn't be any older than about twenty. Still, she probably knew more about dogs than he did, and according to the website the company performed several checks on their carers (that's what they called their walkers and sitters), so he sent her a message as per the company's guidelines, asking her for a meeting.

Lovely, came the instant reply. ***When would you like to meet and what's the address?***

How about today? I'm going out at 2.30, but I can do either before or after. Or tomorrow? He didn't want to leave it until tomorrow, just in case he didn't like the cut of her jib (one of his mum's expressions), or she failed to turn up. Time was critical, and he wouldn't be able to rest until he knew that Poppy was taken care of; it wasn't the puppy's fault that his parents were irresponsible idiots and that he had work on Monday.

I can be with you in an hour?

Great. He sent her his address and leant back, blowing out his cheeks.

Then he sat up straight again as his gaze shot around the living room. The place was a tip. He needed to do some serious tidying up, and a spot of cleaning if he was going to have a visitor and not die of embarrassment. Besides, if this meeting went well, she'd be coming into his house alone all next week. He'd be mortified if she saw it in this state. He wasn't a slob, not that much of one, he told himself; it was just that he'd been so busy at work, and although the term hadn't been a particularly long one, it had been a hard one, what with the A level examinations and the GCSEs, and the younger ones coming up from the primary schools for a visit… He simply hadn't managed to summon the energy to sort the house out when he came home from work.

If nothing came of this meeting, then at least he would have given the house a clean and washed a few shirts. He could do with changing the sheets on his bed too – not that he expected her to go upstairs, because if she needed the loo there was one just off the pantry which was perfectly acceptable. If she ignored the fact that it had a pushbike in it and the vacuum cleaner, that is. And three hubcaps, because he'd had to buy a new set after he'd lost one and by the time he'd put the new ones on he couldn't be bothered to stick the others in the shed. They must have been in the loo for about four months, he realised, therefore he probably hadn't cleaned the smallest room in the house since then, either. He didn't use it, so it hadn't mattered. Until now.

In a fit of embarrassment, he shifted the dog off his lap and onto the sofa, then jumped to his feet. The pup rolled over onto her back, and stretched and yawned, giving him a glimpse of a soft doggy tummy and sharp white teeth. Then she gazed up at him with trusting inquisitive eyes.

At some point during the last sixteen or so hours, Poppy had decided he was OK. Gone was the fearful wary expression, and in its place was a look that Theo could only describe as mischievous.

It was going to be hard to keep an eye on her and clean up at the same time, so he popped her into the kitchen before starting on the living room.

However, no sooner had he closed the door, than

the whimpering and yelping began.

She evidently wasn't happy about being abandoned, even if he was only in the next room, which didn't bode well for the week ahead. If she couldn't tolerate a couple of minutes on her own, then how she was going to cope with a couple of hours was beyond him. Thank goodness the cottage was detached – the thought of his neighbours being able to hear the racket she was making through an adjoining wall made him feel quite anxious.

Having no option other than to ignore her, he popped his headphones on and cranked the music up. He'd start with the living room and hall, then the kitchen, and finally the pantry and downstairs loo. If he had time, he'd tackle the upstairs, he decided, setting to with vigour.

It took longer than he anticipated to give the place a serious clean, because he ended up freeing the pup from her kitcheny prison and trying to keep an eye on her at the same time (using the vacuum cleaner had been a rather fraught experience) long before he'd completed his task. Despite the headphones, he was certain he could hear her mournful cries, and his conscience simply wouldn't let him leave her in such distress, so he'd relented and allowed her to "help" him.

Finally, it was done, and he just had time for another

quick shower before the carer turned up.

When the bell rang, the pair of them were ready and waiting for her.

'Right, then, let's go and meet your new friend,' he told Poppy, picking her up and carrying her into the hall. 'Hi, you must be Josie,' he said as he opened the door. 'I'm Theo and this is the dog.' He held her up for Josie to see.

'Poppy, you said?'

He nodded. 'Come in. Would you like something to drink, tea or coffee?'

'A coffee would be lovely,' she said, stepping past him as he moved to one side to allow her to enter. She hadn't looked at him once, all her attention on the dog. 'She's gorgeous.'

'She is rather,' he agreed, indicating she should go ahead into the living room. He put the dog on the floor. 'Have a seat, I won't be a sec.'

Leaving the door open so he could at least hear if not see what was happening, he headed for the kitchen, listening intently to the carer's soft voice as she spoke to his dog.

Josie Wilde was extremely pretty, even prettier than her photo had suggested, he'd noticed, but maybe not as young as he'd first thought. Late twenties, perhaps? He felt a bit better about her being older, hoping that maturity, responsibility and reliability would go hand-in-hand.

He returned to the living room carrying two mugs of steaming coffee, to find her sitting cross-legged on the floor with the dog in her lap. Both of them seemed quite content with the arrangement.

'She seems to have taken to you,' Theo said, handing her a mug.

Josie took it carefully, holding it away from herself so as not to spill any of the hot liquid on the pup. 'At this age they generally take to anyone,' she said. 'How long have you had her?'

He counted in his head. 'Eighteen hours.'

She gave him a quizzical look. 'Not long, then?'

He sat on one of the armchairs and explained, 'My mum thought it would be a good idea if I had a dog. So she gave me one yesterday evening.' He made a face.

'You don't seem too thrilled.'

'I'm not. She didn't even ask me if I wanted a pet. She just rocked up with the dog, then scarpered off to Harrogate with no thought as to how I'm going to manage next week.'

'Which is why you registered with *The Next Best Thing*?'

'Correct. I only need someone for a week. I'm a teacher see, and school breaks up on Friday.'

'OK, that's fine. Have you made arrangements for September, or are you going to see how this week pans out?'

'I don't need to. I'll have rehomed her by then.'

'I see.' Josie's expression was non-committal, but Theo was certain he heard disapproval in her voice. It practically radiated off her.

'I don't want a dog. Or a cat,' he said, feeling aggrieved. 'Or even a hamster. So the only thing I can do under the circumstances is to find her a new home.' He heard the defensiveness in his tone, but what else was he supposed to do with the animal?

'I suggest that sooner would be better than later,' she said. 'You don't want her getting too attached to you if you intend getting rid of her.'

"Getting rid" sounded awful. It wasn't like that at all, and he resented the way she was making him feel, especially when he thought he was behaving responsibly. 'I'm sure it won't be long before I find someone suitable,' he replied stiffly.

'I'll keep my ear to the ground, if you like. As you say, such a loving, cute little pup will soon be snapped up. What is it you need from a carer?' Suddenly, she was all business.

'She can't go on walks for another week, so I want someone to provide her with some company during the day.' He looked at her hopefully. He was still smarting a bit from her implied criticism, but he was reassured by the fact that she only had the dog's best interests at heart, and he got the impression that she didn't care about offending him and not getting the job; it was the dog who was her main concern.

'Ideally, I'd like to take her to my house,' Josie said, 'but she can't socialise with other dogs yet so I'll have to come to yours. Would you be happy with that?'

He shrugged. 'I don't have much choice,' he said, then realised how churlish he sounded. 'I mean,' he added hastily, 'that's the only option open to me at the moment.'

'I can't have her at mine because I have a dog of my own, and although he's up-to-date with his vaccinations, I wouldn't want to take the risk.'

'I can take her out though, can't I? If I carry her?' He was thinking of taking her with him to the pub. They could sit outside in the beer garden as long as he didn't put her down.

'That's a good idea. If you expose her to a load of different experiences while she's young, the better socialised she'll be and the happier she'll be.'

Theo didn't like to disillusion her that the only reason he wanted to take the dog out was because he fancied a beer with a mate. 'Can you start on Monday?'

'I can. I do have other dogs to see to, but I can fit Poppy in around them. What time do you leave for work?'

'Eight ish.'

'And what time will you be home?'

'Four-forty-five on Monday, three-forty-five the rest of the week.'

'I suggest I pop in twice a day, once in the morning at about ten for an hour, or an hour and a half, then again at about two. That way she's not left on her own for more than two hours at a stretch. If you have a good play with her in the morning before you go to work, and don't let her sleep from the minute she wakes up until the time you leave, then she'll probably be too tired to create much of a fuss when you go. I'll do the same when I call in. Do you want to see any references? My DBS certificate?' She reached for her bag.

'It's OK, I trust that the company has vetted you.'

'They have – every carer has to have a criminal record check and have their identity verified. Are you happy with my suggestion?'

He was. 'I'll fetch you a spare key,' he said. 'Please help yourself to tea and coffee while you're here. And I think I have a biscuit or two in the cupboard.'

'That's very generous of you. If you're happy with the arrangement, you'll need to log in to *The Next Best Thing* to inform them, and I'll do the same to say I've accepted the job. After that, we're good to go.'

'I'll do it as soon as you've left,' he promised, finding her a front door key and handing it to her in exchange for the sleepy puppy.

With Poppy in his arms, he saw Josie out, feeling much better about the whole dog thing now that he'd sorted out Poppy's care.

He found he trusted Josie, and he liked her too. A lot. And it had nothing to do with the fact that she was pretty. Nothing at all.

CHAPTER 5

Theo was hardly aware of the weight of the pup. He was carrying her with one arm, and she was so light it was like holding a bag of feathers. Warm feathers, with a licky tongue and lolling paws, who sometimes squirmed a bit.

What he *was* aware of – acutely aware – were the looks he was getting as he walked along the high street with her.

'Ooh, look at the gorgeous puppy,' a middle-aged lady cried, elbowing her friend in the ribs.

'What did you do that for—? Oh. *Oh my*, that's adorable,' her friend squealed.

The pair of them veered to the side, right into Theo's path, forcing him to stop.

'Can I stroke it?'

'How old is he? She?'

'I've never seen anything so cute in all my life.'

The comments kept coming without respite, barely giving him time to answer. 'Yes. Eleven weeks. It's a she, a girl.'

'Isn't she cute? Can I take her home?' The women's hands were all over the little dog's head, gently stroking her, and the pup wriggled and fidgeted, trying to sniff and lick their fingers at the same time. She was obviously enjoying the attention.

Theo, on the other hand, wasn't so keen. He just wanted to get to the pub and taste that first mouthful of cold, smooth Reverend James.

'Yes, she is cute, and no, you can't take her home,' he replied automatically. Hang on a sec… 'Are you serious?' he asked, thinking furiously. 'About taking her home with you, I mean?'

The woman gave him a strange look. 'Not really. I've got two dogs of my own and they wouldn't like a puppy darting around their feet. They're elderly now, and a youngster would be too much for them.'

'Pity,' Theo said, earning himself another odd look.

The women didn't linger long after that, hurrying away and shooting glances at him over their shoulders as they disappeared down the street.

'Don't worry,' he crooned in Poppy's ear. 'I didn't mean it.' But a little voice wondered if he had meant it. What if one of the women had said yes? Would he have just handed the pup over without a second thought?

No, he decided. He wouldn't have. His conscience wouldn't have allowed it. Poppy's new owner needed to be vetted properly and—

'O.M.G!!! How cute is that?'

A group of three women, probably in their early twenties, came to a halt directly in front of him, forcing him to stop yet again. At this rate he wouldn't get to the pub before last orders.

'What's its name?' the prettiest of the three said, a gooey expression on her face as she stretched out a long-nailed finger to tickle the dog under the chin.

'Poppy,' he replied.

'Ooh, a girl. I prefer girls to boys.'

Theo raised an eyebrow.

'Dogs, I mean,' she giggled. 'I prefer girl dogs to boy dogs.' She flashed him a smile and fluttered her eyelashes. 'When it comes to lurve, I like men.' Her gaze met his and her teeth caught her bottom lip suggestively. 'How old is she?'

Theo shuffled uneasily before he answered, wondering if the woman was flirting with him, or whether he was imagining it. 'Eleven weeks.' He might just have to make a sign to go around the dog's neck to save him the bother of answering the same questions over and over again.

'What is she?' Another of the girls asked. She flicked a lock of long blonde hair over her shoulder.

'A Cockapoo,' he said, eliciting a fit of giggles from all three.

'That's just up your street,' the third girl cried, nudging the one who had batted her eyelashes at him.

Theo didn't know what to say. 'Erm, right, I'd, er, better be off,' he muttered.

'Aw, we've gone and embarrassed him,' the prettiest one said. 'Don't worry, hun; it's your dog I'm after, not your bod.' Her eyes swept over him from head to foot. 'But, then again…'

He blushed furiously. She *was* flirting with him!

'He's blushing,' she teased, and the hand that had been caressing the dog, moved to his arm. 'You're safe. I won't tell your girlfriend if you won't.'

'I haven't got a girlfriend,' he said, without thinking.

'A wife, then?'

'Er, no.'

'Why not? Single, hunky, and with a really, really cute dog?'

'Dunno. Look, I've got to go.'

'Don't tell me – you're going to see a man about a dog!' She squealed with laughter and Theo winced.

She might be pretty, but she was too in-your-face and loud for his liking. The third young woman, on the other hand, the shy one who had yet to say a word—

'Ooh, Mummy, I want that puppy!' A demanding child's voice cut through his discomfort as the three women were supplanted by a little girl in pigtails wearing a pink tutu, a princess crown and a pair of sparkly fairy wings. She was eyeing Poppy with an avaricious expression, and dragging her mum across the pavement into his path.

So once again, Theo had only taken a couple of steps before he was stopped this time by what looked to be a five-year-old and her long-suffering, eye-rolling mum.

'You can't have it, Sukie,' her mother said, trying to drag the child away.

Sukie held her ground, digging her heels in and crossing her arms. 'I want it.'

'It belongs to this nice man. You wouldn't want to take it off him and make him cry, would you?'

The child shrugged. 'I don't care.'

'Remember what we've talked about? Being nice to others and considering their feelings?'

Sukie gave her mum a disdainful glare. 'You said I could have a puppy, and I want that one.' She pointed at Poppy and the dog flinched back as the little finger came rather too close to the pup's eyes.

'Sorry,' the child's mum mouthed at him, and he wondered what she was apologising for.

Having an obnoxious spoilt brat for a daughter, perhaps?

An ear-splitting scream tore through the air, and the

little girl jumped up and down in a fit of temper. Ah, so that's what the apology was for.

Swiftly, he covered Poppy's ears, dodged around the temper tantrum in pink, and hurried on his way.

By the time he arrived at the Cardinal's Trumpet, he was exhausted, and his nerves were frayed. His journey had been interrupted several more times by people (mostly of the female gender) wanting to pet, pat and stroke the pup, and demanding to know her age, her breed, how big she'd grow, whether they could hold her, take her home, and otherwise drool and coo over her. He wasn't sure which one of them was the most shell-shocked – him or the dog.

And to top it all off, he was late he realised, as he peered through one of the pub's windows to see Jenson already seated at a table, with a pint of golden nectar in front of him which was already half-empty.

He rapped on the window.

No response. Not even from the group of lads sitting directly behind it.

He knocked again.

One of them eventually turned around, scowling. His lips moved, 'What?'

Theo pointed at Jenson and mouthed, 'Can you tell him I'm out here?'

More scowling.

'Please. I can't come in.' He held Poppy up.

Immediately the youth's face was transformed into a smile. He nodded, turned away from the window and leant forward to say something to Jenson. Theo watched Jenson look at the youth, then at the window.

Theo held the pup up higher.

Jenson shook his head, picked up his pint and stood up. He disappeared from view for a few seconds, before reappearing at the pub's door.

'I couldn't leave her on her own for too long,' Theo said by way of an apology, 'so I brought her with me.' He'd also brought a small plastic bowl, some poo bags, a length of kitchen roll, a packet of wet wipes and some puppy food. It was like taking a baby out, he'd thought earlier as he packed his small rucksack, marvelling at the amount of stuff he needed to take with him. 'We can sit in the beer garden,' he added.

Jenson sighed. 'Take my pint and go find a table. What are you having?'

'Reverend James, please.' Theo did as he was told and found an empty table.

It was rather pleasant sitting outside in the sun and he turned his face up to it, revelling in its warmth. The pub's garden was surrounded by high stone walls with assorted plants growing up their sides, the colour and perfume of their flowers making the place seem a bit cottage gardenish and rather peaceful – if you ignored the smokers sitting on the benches and the raucous laughter coming from a group of young women on the table nearest to him. They were undoubtedly out for a good time and it appeared that most of them were already three sheets to the wind.

He caught the eye of an attractive girl a few feet away, who was smiling broadly at him, and he smiled back – until he realised it was his dog she was grinning at not him, and that her male companion didn't seem half as friendly. And the bloke looked positively cross when his wife or girlfriend got to her feet and walked over to him.

Theo smiled again, this time a little uncertainly. He knew what she was here for, but did her other half realise it was the dog she fancied and not the man who was holding it?

'Aww, he's so cute,' the girl exclaimed.

If he had a pound for every time he'd heard that today… 'Yeah, she is, isn't she? Her name is Poppy, she's eleven weeks old and she's a Cockapoo,' he said, anticipating the questions which were sure to follow the "cute" statement.

'That's a cross between a Cocker spaniel and a poodle, isn't it? Can I stroke her?'

He nodded. 'Apparently, so. I don't know much about dogs.'

'What made you decide to have one of these? My sister has got one, and it's a bit mad, like, stupidly lively.'

'I didn't—' He was about to say that his mother had presented him with the dog, but then a thought occurred to him. 'Have you seen the film John Wick?'

'Is that the one where an assassin retired because he met the love of his life, then she died? But before she passed away, she arranged to have a puppy sent to him after her death so he had something else to live for?'

'Yep. That's the one...' He trailed off and left her to draw her own conclusion.

Satisfyingly, she arrived at the one he wanted. 'Aww, poor you. That's so sad, yet so lovely.'

'Angel?' It was her husband or boyfriend calling.

Theo checked out her left hand. Boyfriend.

'I'd best go,' she sighed, giving the dog a final tickle behind the ears. Poppy wriggled with delight.

After the girl had returned to her own table and Poppy kept on wriggling, Theo realised that she wanted to be put down, and he also had a good idea of the reason. She needed a wee.

He hadn't thought this through, had he? If he put her on the ground to do the necessary, then he was putting her at risk of catching something. The vaccines may well have taken effect, but he didn't want to risk it, so as soon as Jenson returned with their drinks, Theo explained what he was about to do and darted off to the loo, the dog still in his arms.

It wasn't ideal, and it wasn't particularly hygienic, but as soon as he popped her on the tiled floor of the gents' toilets, Poppy made a puddle, and Theo was positive he could see the relief on her little face. He swiftly cleaned it up and washed her paws too, before going back outside.

'Mate, you're acting like she's a kid, not a dog,' Jenson drawled, a bemused expression on his face.

'Speaking of kids, how's Bella?'

'Huge. Grumpy. Can't talk about anything other than baby stuff. And she's still got five weeks to go.' Jenson downed the remainder of his first pint and started on his second. Theo had barely taken a sip out of his and Jenson caught him staring. 'What? I'm making the most of this,' he said. 'When the baby arrives, I probably won't be able to pop out to the pub on a Saturday afternoon.' He sounded regretful. 'Stick to dogs, mate. They're much less hassle, from what I've been told.'

'I don't intend to, either.' Theo rearranged the pup so that she was sitting comfortably on his lap. 'I'm going to have to find this little thing a new home. What time have I got for a dog? I work full time, for God's sake.'

Jenson smirked. 'Call that full time? You've got it cushy – three months off a year and a three-thirty finish every day.'

'Don't start.' Theo warned. 'Just because the kids can sod off home at that time, doesn't mean to say the staff can. There are meetings for this, that and the other, parents' evenings, open evenings, bloody twilight training sessions, and that's without the—'

'Marking!' Jenson chorused. 'You ought to try working in the real world. I don't get home until six most nights, and I only have twenty-two days holiday a year.'

'You ought to try teaching 10.3,' Theo muttered, but before he could expand on his comment, they were interrupted by a squeal of feminine voices.

The puppy had been spotted once more.

'Oh, my, God. Look at that cute puppy,' one of the women on the table next to them cried. 'Gimme, gimme, gimme.' She reached out, making grabby motions with her hands.

Poppy's ears pricked up and her tail began to wag. Theo had yet to see a human whom the dog didn't like. Apart from him last night, that is. But now that she'd settled down, she seemed much happier.

One of the girl's friends got up and tottered over to him on heels so high Theo wondered how she kept her balance. Her attention was on the puppy. 'Is it a him or a her?'

'A her. Poppy. Eleven weeks. Cockapoo.' He was getting seriously fed up of repeating himself.

'She's gorgeous. Can I hold her?'

For some reason, Theo found himself reluctant to hand her over. 'Um, she's not had all her injections yet, so I'm trying to limit her interaction with people and other dogs in case she catches anything.' It wasn't a total lie.

'Are you saying I've got a disease, or something?' the young woman asked indignantly, and Theo was about to get flustered and try to explain what he meant, when he noticed the gleam in her eye and the upward curve of her full lips.

She was teasing.

'I totally understand,' she said, letting him off the hook. 'We've always had dogs, so I know the score.' She was looking at him expectantly.

'What dog have you got?' he asked, just as he was expected to.

'We've got two, an Airedale and a Boston terrier. Pair of little gits, they are. Last week one of them chewed the toe off my favourite trainers. I couldn't tell them off as I didn't know which one of them did it.'

She didn't sound too bothered, and he guessed she loved her pooches too much to be cross with them for long.

'You wait until she starts teething,' she continued. 'You'll spend most of your time taking things out of her mouth. Oh, sorry, you probably know all this already.'

'I don't actually. This is the first time I've owned a dog.' And he wouldn't be owning one for much longer either, if he had his way.

'Is it? That's lovely!'

Theo wasn't so sure about that.

'Look, if you need to know anything – and I'm sure you don't – give me a call. You've probably got loads of people you can ask for advice, but just in case…' She grabbed a beer mat, pulled a lipstick out of her pocket and proceeded to scrawl over it.

Theo was a dab hand at reading upside-down handwriting; it kind of went with the job. Her name was Taylor and she'd added her phone number.

'You can call me anytime,' she said. 'Ask me anything…'

'Um, OK, thanks.' He picked up the beer mat and waved it about. 'I'll… er… be certain to ring you if I have any questions.'

'Make sure you do.' She sent him a long, lingering look before returning to her friends, who began giggling and nudging her, shooting him knowing looks as they did so.

Jenson was leaning back in his seat, arms folded, his eyebrows raised and a grin on his face.

'What?' Theo asked.

'Bloody hell, mate, you've got a right babe magnet

there! Can I borrow it?'

I don't follow…'

'The dog! Birds can't get enough of her, you lucky sod. I wish I'd known that little secret before I got hitched. It would have saved me hours and hours of going to nightclubs.'

'You think…?'

'Course I damn well do! They're falling all over you.'

'They're falling over the dog,' Theo pointed out.

'That one wasn't.' Jenson jerked his head towards the group of girls. 'She gave you her number as sweet as a nut. None of this nonsense of having to chat her up and buy her drinks all night. You're in there, mate.'

'I am?' Theo was rather bemused. He hadn't been "in there" for a very long time indeed. In fact, his luck had been so poor in the "in there" department, that he'd given up trying a couple of years ago. These days, he stuck to going out with his coupled-up mates for the occasional pint or two and keeping himself to himself, or staying in and watching Netflix – without the chill. The last woman he'd tried to chat up had been a supply teacher (history department) who had flirted outrageously with him during the time she was at his school, but who'd refused any and all subsequent offers of meeting up for a drink or "going out for a meal sometime". Afterwards he'd found out she was living with a long-term partner.

'You are so right in there. Don't phone her too soon, though,' Jenson advised. 'Treat 'em mean and keep 'em keen.'

'Does that work?' Theo wanted to know. He'd never particularly wanted to treat anyone mean.

Jenson tapped the side of his nose with his finger. 'Take it from one who's been there, done that. How do you think I nabbed Bella?'

Theo had to concede the point. Bella was gorgeous, well out of Jenson's league, and Jenson had received endless amounts of ribbing to that effect, all his mates wondering how he'd managed to bag someone so lovely. Jenson always claimed it was due to the size of his manhood, but Theo had seen him in the showers after a footie match and he knew there was nothing exceptional in that regard.

'You wanna hang on to that mutt for a while, if that's the attention you're getting,' Jenson advised. 'Not for ever – because, let's face it, puppies are only puppies for a short time and it'll soon lose the cute factor – but I'd keep it for a couple of weeks, if I were you. You can get into loads of knickers with that on the end of a lead. Take her, for instance.' He jerked his head at Taylor. 'She's yours for the asking. You lucky sod.'

Theo thought about it. Admittedly, he'd had more female attention this afternoon than he'd ever had in his whole life before. OK, not him – it was the dog who was attracting the attention – but he was benefitting from it, and he'd already been given a girl's number. How many more numbers (and potential dates) could he get before Poppy had lost her puppy cuteness?

Maybe Jenson had a point…?

CHAPTER 6

It worked! Theo squinted at his mobile phone in amazement. It had been Jenson's idea that Theo installed a camera in the kitchen, so he could keep an eye on Poppy when he wasn't there.

'Use an old mobile,' Jenson had said. 'It works just fine. I should know, because I've tried it. Bella's not too keen, but enough is enough. She wanted to spend a hundred-and-thirty quid on a baby monitor! I nearly had a fit. Asked her what the hell she wanted a baby monitor for. You can hear my sister's kid from four streets away – you don't need a sodding monitor for that. But she insisted, so when I was looking online for something cheaper, I came across this site that lets you use an old mobile phone as a camera, and you can view it on the phone you're currently using. Genius, I thought, and it's free. Bella was none too happy – only the best for our baby, she said. By "best", she means the most expensive. I'm sticking to my guns this time though, especially since I tried it out and it works just fine.'

So yesterday, after Theo had returned from the pub with a sleepy pup in his arms, he'd dug out one of his old phones and charged it up. This morning he'd downloaded the app to both phones and followed a simple set of instructions to get the whole thing set up in a matter of minutes.

Brilliant!

He was able to see everything that went on in his kitchen, and he could see a little bit of the garden too, and he spent rather more time than was necessary walking around the room and viewing himself on his phone. He'd be able to view Poppy quite clearly, and see how she reacted when the dog sitter arrived.

Not that he was intending to use it to spy on Josie – because he wasn't, and it was only set up in the kitchen anyway and not installed in every room in the house – but it would certainly come in handy to check that the puppy wasn't getting too distressed when he was out, or worse, destroying his kitchen. He could probably do with a new one, those units having been there for at least fifteen years before his gran died and left him the cottage, but he didn't want to be forced into such a major purchase by the actions of a small dog.

He'd tell Josie about the camera tomorrow. He didn't think if fair or right to aim a lens at her without her knowing it was there; he'd leave her a note next to the kettle where she couldn't fail to miss it.

Thinking about Josie's visit in the morning led to him thinking about Josie herself. There was something about her that made him think he could trust her. That might be because Poppy had taken to her, but then the pup seemed to take to most people, so that wasn't an accurate gauge of character. She'd happily accepted all the petting and fussing yesterday, although she had slept for hours afterwards, then had woken up in the evening and hadn't wanted to sleep again for ages.

Theo was exhausted. This was worse than having a baby in the house, but his only consolation was that all the websites about puppy care had told him to persevere because the crying at night stage wouldn't last for more than a few nights.

There she was right now sleeping happily in her basket while he'd been fiddling around with the camera, and he was tempted to wake her up in the hope that he'd get a bit more sleep tonight. But the peace and quiet won, and he crept into the living room and sank onto the sofa with a weary sigh.

Debating whether to switch the TV on, he decided against it in case it disturbed the pup (who he was watching avidly on his phone, the novelty not yet having worn off), he brought up *The Next Best Thing* site to check that everything was OK for Josie's first session.

Seeing that everything was fine, he scrolled around on the internet for a while looking at the footie scores and the results of yesterday's cricket, when without thinking about what he was doing he typed Josie Wilde into the search bar.

There were a number of hits; Twitter, Facebook, LinkedIn and other sites, none of which he was on, not wanting to have his details splashed all over the internet for his resourceful pupils to discover. WhatsApp was his limit, along with the occasional notification from a popular newsfeed site.

Curious, he clicked on Twitter and saw that there were more people called Josie Wilde than he could shake a stick at. He examined a few of them (more than a few, if he was honest) before he finally found her.

It was no surprise to see that nearly all her tweets and retweets were about dogs, with some cutesy pictures of other animals thrown in. Crumble, her spaniel, featured heavily, although there were a couple of posts which were non-animal related and Theo zeroed in on those.

In every single shot she looked happy. Most of them showed her laughing, sometimes with her arm around a friend (female, he noted), sometimes raising a glass, or eating a meal, or on the beach, or in the snow… No matter where she was or who she was with, she appeared to find joy in the moment.

He briefly considered whether she was putting it on for the camera, but he didn't think so. Her smile always reached her eyes, and there didn't appear to be much in the way of posing either. No trout-pout, no silly hand-gestures, no views taken from above where the angle made women look as though they had massive foreheads. She just looked natural. Normal. Happy. Beautiful.

A flash of envy shot through him and he narrowed his eyes. Nah, she must be acting. No one could be that joyous all the time. Heck, he had trouble being joyous any of the time. Maybe he should try doing snow angels (it was the wrong time of year for it right now) or splash through the waves, kicking up the surf? Maybe he wasn't doing the right things to make him as happy as Josie appeared to be.

He wasn't *unhappy*, though. Was he? He didn't think so. He quite liked his life the way it was; ordered, predictable, with no nasty surprises. He loved his cottage and the independence it gave him (thanks, Gran, wherever you are), he loved… he loved… um…

That was it for the love section of his life. He certainly couldn't say that he loved his job. Endured, tolerated, or put up with, would be more accurate words to use.

He slumped back, the knowledge taking him by surprise. When had he gone from being enthusiastic about his job and loving the fact that he could make a difference to young lives, that he could help influence and shape the minds of the pupils in his care, to trudging through the days and longing for the weekends? He couldn't pin-point a time. Or an event. The erosion if his love of teaching had taken place over the weeks, terms, and years of too much paperwork, stupid, pointless and constant changes to the curriculum, the attitude of parents, the attitude of the kids themselves, and of society as a whole.

Maybe he should have a serious rethink about his choice of career?

And, while he was at it, he should take a good hard look at his life in general. He could accept that he didn't love his job the way he once had, that work for him was simply somewhere that he was forced to go to on a daily basis in order to pay the bills. Like most of the people he knew, he worked to live and not lived to work. But that's where his argument came undone. He wasn't doing much in the way of living outside of work, either.

Take last weekend, for instance. What had he done? A smidgeon of housework which consisted of washing a couple of shirts because he had no clean ones left in the wardrobe, watched a whole series of Life on Mars (for the second time), and went to his parents' house for Sunday dinner. Oh, and don't forget the marking – the never-ending, soul-destroying marking.

He had no life to speak of. If his life was to be displayed on Twitter in a series of photos the way Josie's was, it would consist of multiple shots of him slumped despondently over the desk in his classroom, or slumped wearily in his armchair at home. He could guarantee that he would not be smiling in any of them; grimacing maybe…

Oh, dear God, he was turning into a grumpy old git, and he was only thirty-three!

He seriously didn't want to admit that maybe, just maybe, his mum had a point and that he seriously did need livening up a bit.

Theo stared thoughtfully at his phone. Poppy was still slumbering peacefully in her basket, and his heart went out to her. He couldn't keep her and he felt as guilty as hell for that, but he was nevertheless grateful to the pup. In less than forty-eight hours, she'd shown him what life should be like – full of colour and joy – and not the greyed-out, scaled-down version he currently existed in.

Giving silent thanks to the dog, he vowed he'd find her the best, most loving home he possibly could.

CHAPTER 7

Monday mornings sucked. Except for those lovely Mondays when he didn't have to get up for work and the day signified the start of a school-free week. Theo liked *those* Mondays. This Monday wasn't one of them, but it was the next best type of Monday – the start of the last week of a term. Thank God for that! If he had to endure another week in work, he thought he might just scream. Or grizzle a bit, at the very least.

Today he could add tired and guilty to the "why I hate Mondays" list. Poppy had woken up in the night *again* – three times to be exact – which was why he felt like a fully-paid-up member of the walking dead; and he felt guilty for having to leave her on her own even if it was only for a couple of hours. He'd been up since the crack of dawn – not by choice, but because Poppy had been yipping and yelping – playing with her to wear her out. But he had a horrible suspicion that he'd only succeeded in wearing himself out. The pup still looked fresh and raring to go, whereas all he wanted to do was to go back to bed and forget about school.

Unfortunately, that wasn't an option.

Steeling himself to leave, he picked the dog up, sniffing the gorgeous puppy scent of her, and cuddled her close.

'I'm sorry, little one. I wish I could stay home with you today,' he murmured into her soft fur. To be fair, he felt like staying home most days and not just because he felt horrid at leaving the pup on her own. But today was a whole lot worse than usual.

As she gazed up at him with dark-chocolate eyes, his heart constricted.

'Get a grip,' he muttered. 'It's only a dog.' It wasn't as though he was leaving a baby on his or her own for the day. And anyway, Josie was coming in to see to her, so Poppy would only be alone for a couple of hours.

With the pup held under one arm, he scrabbled around in his bag for some paper on which to leave the dog-sitter a note telling her to help herself to tea and coffee, that there were biscuits in the tin in the cupboard, and that there was a camera in the kitchen.

Giving the pup a kiss on her fluffy head, he swiftly deposited her on the tiled floor and made a dash for the door, his stomach turning over. He didn't want to do this to her, and he felt sorry for having to leave.

Poppy – well aware what the process signified because Theo did exactly the same thing when he shut her in the kitchen at night – scampered after him. She was faster than he was, and beat him to the door with ease, getting caught between his feet and nearly tripping him up.

'Damn and blast!' he cried, as he almost went headfirst into the door frame, banging his shoulder against it instead, the sudden pain making him wince. That hurt.

With a resigned sigh he picked her up again, feeling that he would be the one to get fed up with this little game sooner than the dog would.

'Stay,' he commanded, popping her into her basket and raising a finger in the air to show her that he meant what he said.

Poppy cocked her head to one side, regarding him solemnly.

He took one step backwards. Then another.

The dog tilted her head to the other side, but at least she didn't make a move to get out of her basket.

Backing away slowly, he inched towards the door. When he thought he stood a fighting chance of getting through it, he made a mad dash, his feet skidding on the tiles as he shot through the opening and pulled the door shut behind him.

He leant against the wood, breathing hard. It was

only ten-past eight and he felt as though he'd already done an hour in the gym.

The door rattled as the small dog launched herself at it, and Theo winced. It was best if he got out of the house and began his working day, because if he stood there any longer listening to her pathetic desolate whimpering, he might just phone in sick and be done with it.

Cross with himself for feeling this way about a stupid dog, he stomped down the hall, yanked his front door open and slammed it shut behind him.

Bloody hell, he hated Mondays.

And his mood didn't improve when he drove into the school's car park and saw a huddle of Year 10 pupils smoking around the back of one of the metal boxes which was supposed to be a make-shift classroom.

He knew he should confront them and at the very least confiscate their smoking paraphernalia (he should also by rights report them to the senior leadership team) but he simply didn't have the will or the energy for argy-bargy at this time in the morning. If the little darlings wanted to slowly kill themselves, that was up to them he reasoned, as he turned a blind eye and let them get on with it, pretending to be engrossed in his phone.

Unable to stop himself once he'd thought of his

phone, he felt compelled to check the camera.

Poppy was pacing around the kitchen, head down, tail down, looking forlorn, and he wished he was there to comfort her. He mightn't be keeping her, but he hated to think she was distressed at being on her own. Checking his watch, he saw it wasn't quite half-past eight yet, and there were still two hours to go before Josie put in an appearance.

Oh, well, he couldn't be worrying about it now; he had a five-minute meeting with his fellow tutors, then his tutor group to see to. Mondays were uniform check days and he really, really disliked having to tell a bunch of teenage girls that they had to take their make-up off, remove their nose, eyebrow, or chin piercings (sometimes all three), and to not come to school with purple, blue, pink or green hair. The purple looked quite nice, he reluctantly admitted, but the green made the fourteen-year-old who had been wearing it last week resemble an alien, in his opinion. But what did he know about fashion, the pupil had pointed out when he confronted her, staring meaningfully at his worn jacket and mismatched brown trousers.

He took the opportunity to swiftly glance at his phone between tutorial and the start of the first lesson, to discover that the pup was still pacing. Every now and again she would cease her aimless wandering to throw herself at the door and cry. Just as swiftly he exited the app, his heart twisting. Dear God, this was worse than having a child. He was worrying about the dog just as much as if she was a human baby being left in a crèche.

'Sir, why do you keep sniffing your jacket? Are you some kind of weirdo?'

The class, who had filed into his room unnoticed while he fretted over the dog, burst into mean laughter.

He frowned at them. Had he been doing that? He realised he had – the scent of the pup, sweet and almost milky, was on his clothes, and he'd been unconsciously sniffing his lapel.

'I've got a dog,' he said, by way of explanation, before he realised it made him sound even stranger than the class already thought he was, when they pulled faces and eyed each other. 'I thought she might have been a bit sick on me,' he added, trying to rescue the situation before he lost total control of them. Teenagers in a group were like a pack of hyenas – they could sense weakness a mile away and would be quick to exploit it.

'What? Like a baby? My little sister barfs all over my mum when she's had a feed. It's disgusting. I won't let her anywhere near me,' one of the girls said with an exaggerated grimace.

'Yeah, a bit like that,' Theo replied vaguely, not wanting to get drawn into a discussion about babies, bottles and being sick. You never knew where something like that might lead to, and he didn't want to hear about underage drinking and any subsequent throwing up or other mishaps. He'd have to report it, for one thing...

'Right, statistics and probability,' he announced, receiving a chorus of groans in response, and a whole wave of sighs and eye-rolling. He felt like telling them that he didn't want to teach it almost as much as they didn't want to learn it, but he held his tongue. And he meant "almost", because there was one lad at the back who was an absolute whizz at maths, and he made the whole lesson worthwhile. The kid kept himself to himself, knuckled down and simply got on with it, grasping the concept of whatever Theo was striving to instil with ease, his mind open and curious and wired the right way to understand maths. Theo didn't care what the experts said, some kids were naturally better at some subjects than others, and this one happened to be particularly good at maths.

To Theo's intense relief he had a free lesson next, and he made a mad dash for the staff room, where he made a much needed cup of coffee and sank into one of the battered chairs to study his phone.

This time when he looked, Poppy wasn't pacing and neither was she looking forlorn.

She was cuddled in the arms of Josie and was

showering the woman's face with frantic kisses. He could clearly hear the little noises she was making. Poppy, that was, not the dog sitter. Josie wasn't making little squeaks, but she was speaking softly to the pup in a reassuring murmur whose meaning he couldn't quite catch.

No matter; whatever she was saying, it did the trick. Josie was sitting cross-legged on his kitchen floor, the dog now curled on her lap and staring up at her adoringly, and Theo was pierced by an unexpected and totally unwelcome bolt of envy.

He didn't think Poppy had stared at him in the same way. Not even once, and he was the one looking after her. But, then again, he was also the one who had abandoned her in the kitchen on a regular basis; three times over the course of the past few nights, and then once today. No wonder she must think Josie was her salvation.

He watched the woman get slowly and carefully to her feet, trying not to disturb the puppy too much as she picked her up, and he saw her read his note.

She looked around, finally spotting the camera, and gave him a cheery wave. 'She's fine,' Josie mouthed, unaware that his old phone could pick up sound. Both ways. If he pressed a button his end, he could talk to her. But that was weird, and he'd already been called that once today. He didn't need his dog sitter to think he was sitting there ogling her. Although that was exactly what he appeared to be doing.

'I'm looking at my *dog*,' he said, aloud.

'Are you talking to me?' a female voice asked, and he nearly jumped out of his skin.

For a second, he thought Josie must have heard him, before he realised that an unfamiliar woman was huddled in the far corner of the staff room, her coat on and a shell-shocked expression on her face. He didn't recognise her and guessed she must be a supply teacher.

'Are you covering Mr Donald's drama class?' he asked kindly.

The woman didn't look more than twenty-two or - three and she appeared to be very nervous. 'Yes. That's me. A drama teacher. A not very good one,' she added and promptly burst into tears.

Theo winced, wondering what he was supposed to do. Should he put his arm around her and try to comfort her, or would that be regarded as something less savoury than was intended. You had to be so careful these days to ensure that anything said, not said, or implied, wasn't taken the wrong way, but he couldn't just sit there watching her bawl her eyes out and do nothing, because he might then come across as a heartless git.

See, he thought, this is why he didn't bother much

with the opposite sex. It had the potential to become too complicated, especially in a work situation.

'10.3?' he hazarded a guess.

'7.1,' she sniffled.

'*Really?*' By the end of their first academic year, the Year 7 kids had generally found their feet, but not to the extent that they'd make a supply teacher weep. Give them a couple more years, though…

'They were doing free expression, and I told them they could be anything they wanted to be and the rest of the class had to guess.' She dug a tissue out of an enormous bag and blew into it.

Oh dear, she wasn't all that long out of teacher training was she, as he could just imagine the scenes that probably would have ensued, even for a top set like 7.1. 'When did you qualify?'

'I've just finished, and I'm doing some supply work while I look for a job. Is it that obvious?'

'Um, yeah, sorry. But don't worry, we've all been there. It comes with experience, and with you being so young—'

'I'm thirty-one. Not that young. And I used to boss workmen around in a previous life. You'd think I could handle a bunch of eleven and twelve-year-olds.'

He laughed. 'Controlling kids and classroom management is a whole different ballgame to working with adults,' he told her. 'Just think of them as wild animals in school blazers, and you won't go far wrong.'

The woman wiped her eyes.' Isn't that a bit cynical?'

'Wait until you've been teaching for as long as I have,' he warned. 'I'm Theo, by the way. Maths.'

'Robyn; with a Y. Drama and performing arts.' She gave him a small hesitant smile.

'So, what made you decide to go into teaching?' he asked.

'Am Dram. I'm an active member of my local amateur dramatics club. I do the stage direction.' She shrugged. 'I thought I was fairly good at it.'

'I'm sure you are. And when you get yourself a permanent job, then I'm sure your school will be delighted to have you put on plays and stuff.' He wasn't sure what the "stuff" entailed, but he knew how excited the head teacher in his school became whenever Mr Donald announced that he was thinking of doing some kind of school show. The parents seemed to like it and it was good PR for the school. Apparently, it showed the community that Robert Crouch High School wasn't just about detentions and exam results.

Theo's attention wandered back to his phone. This time, Josie was nowhere to be seen, but he could hear her voice and what he had come to recognise as the dog's play-growls. He smiled, thinking that at least she was wearing the little blighter out.

Abruptly, he saw the dog sitter dart into the kitchen,

the pup held at arms' length as she hastened to unlock the back door. He watched her swiftly deposit the pup outside, then heard her cry, 'Good girl, there's a good, clever girl,' and he guessed that Poppy had done her business outside.

'New puppy,' he said, noticing Robyn's curiosity. 'Camera. See?' He turned his phone screen around.

'Is that your wife?'

'What? *Her?* No, no way, I'm not married.'

'Sorry, I just assumed… Your girlfriend is pretty. And so is your dog. Cute. Not pretty. Um…'

'She's not my girlfriend,' Theo explained. 'She's my dog sitter.'

'Ah, I see. Well, they do say that the summer is the best time to get a dog because of the house-training thing, and with you being a teacher you can spend all summer with it.'

Theo debated whether to explain his intention to rehome Poppy, but decided against it. He was pleased he hadn't said anything when Robyn, who was rather attractive with her mass of blonde curly hair clouding about her face and her large blue eyes, said, 'I adore dogs. She's not very old, is she? She's so cute.'

Ooh, he could get used to this, he thought. Here was another woman who was bowled over by the puppy. 'Eleven weeks. Her name is Poppy.'

'I love nothing better than cuddling a puppy.

They're so gorgeous at that age.'

Theo looked back at his phone to see Josie doing precisely that, and another flash of envy shot through him. By rights, he should be the one at home cuddling his dog, not Josie. But he still wasn't certain why he felt this way – was it because he wished he was at home regardless of whether there was a dog in it or not? Or was it because his dog sitter had a job that allowed her to play with puppies all day, which could hardly be classed as a real job, could it?

The buzzer sounded, indicating the start of the next lesson. 'I'd better be off,' he said. 'Will you be all right?'

'I'm sure I will be. It's just a bit of a culture shock going from being a trainee teacher one minute to being responsible for a whole class all by yourself the next. Maybe I'll see you at lunch?'

She didn't look OK, though. She looked petrified, and he couldn't help feeling a prickle of concern about her.

'Not today, I'm on duty, but I'll be in here at break tomorrow.'

She gave him a small smile, and he could have sworn that she was blushing, despite her worried expression.

However, it wasn't her worried face that kept him company until home time; it was Josie Wilde's blissfully happy one that he couldn't seem to get out of his mind.

CHAPTER 8

Theo felt tears prick behind his eyes and he blinked them away in confusion. What on earth was wrong with him? Anyone would think he'd not seen a dog before. The fact that this one belonged to him (temporarily) and was absolutely ecstatic to see him (so ecstatic that she'd widdled on the floor) should not have made a scrap of difference.

But never before had anyone shown such unbridled joy at being with him and it pulled at his heart. He wasn't in the nicest of moods, he didn't look his best – who would, after three nights of broken sleep? – and he probably stank of the teenage hormones which saturated the school along with the smell of feet and boiled cabbage. The cabbage smell was intrinsic to the school, and no matter what the canteen was serving for lunch cabbage fumes wafted along the corridors and seeped into classrooms.

Yet Poppy was so delighted to see him that she had peed a little. And now she was scrabbling at his legs, begging to be picked up.

When he obliged, his nose sinking into the fluff on the top of her head, she made the cutest little happy noises he'd ever heard.

She smelt a little different to the way she had this morning he thought, as he cuddled her, and he realised it must be Josie's perfume. It was sweet and light, with undertones of flowers. It suited the pup and he wondered if he should ask Josie what it was so he could buy some and spray a little on the dog every day.

'I'm back now,' he crooned. 'It's OK, little one, I'm here. Are you hungry? Are you? I expect you are.' He popped her back down on the floor, and she immediately stood on her hind legs, front paws reaching up. 'I can't sort your dinner out when I'm holding you,' he protested with a chuckle. 'Don't you want some yummy chicken?' He held up a pouch of puppy food for her to see, but she ignored it, more interested in him than her dinner.

Relenting, he crouched down and Poppy immediately crawled onto his knees. 'Can I at least take my jacket off?' he asked, but evidently she wasn't keen on him doing anything that involved her not being in his arms.

'I can't carry you all the time,' he told her, laughing

at her antics. 'What will happen when you get too big to—?'

Gumtree! He still hadn't put an advert on the site, and the longer he left it the harder it would be, he realised. He was already starting to get attached to the little creature and he'd only had her three days. What if three days turned into three weeks? The sooner he found a lovely new home for her, the better it would be for both of them, because she was unquestionably bonding with him, too.

When she finally wriggled, indicating that she'd had enough of being cuddled for now, Theo gently put her down, and sorted her out with some supper. While she was eating, her tail wagging nonstop, he cleaned up the puppy pads, quickly disinfected the floor and replaced them with fresh pads.

Mindful of what he'd read online concerning the swift connection between putting food in one end of a puppy and movement at the other end shortly afterwards, he didn't bother getting changed out of his work clothes. The second she'd hoovered up the last morsel of food, he opened the door to the garden and encouraged her to follow him outside.

Tentatively, she put one paw on the step, then looked up at him with huge questioning eyes.

'It's OK, you're allowed out here. There haven't been any other doggos in this garden since….' He shrugged. 'I dunno, forever.' His grandmother hadn't had a dog, and she'd lived in the cottage for decades.

'Doggos?' he said out loud. 'Did I just say "doggos"?' Theo winced. He was starting to morph into a teenage girl. If any of his mates had heard, he'd have the piss taken out of him for weeks. Years, even. He'd be calling her a "pupper" or a "floof" next, if he wasn't careful. His mum should have bought him something a bit more macho, because this little ball of cuteness was doing nothing for his image.

Although Poppy *was* doing something for his attractiveness to the opposite sex, he acknowledged as he recalled the reaction of females of all ages to the pup on Saturday. And he still had that woman's number somewhere; then there was Robyn at school…

'There's a clever girl!' he cried, spying Poppy, who had ventured onto the patio without him noticing, and was doing her business. 'What a good girl! Who's a good girl, then.' he raved, almost hopping up and down with excitement. A few more sessions like this, and she'd soon get the idea.

After cleaning the mess up (there seemed to be a great deal of mess-cleaning when you owned a dog, he gathered) he took her upstairs with him so he could change into more casual clothes, popping her onto his bed while he did so. Keeping a close eye on her in case she wandered too close to the edge, he pulled on a pair of cut-offs and an old T-shirt, then slipped his feet into some deck shoes. After he'd taken a photo or two of her for the advert, he intended to take her to the park. Not that she would have any actual exercise (he'd have to carry her) but he was mindful of Josie's advice that Poppy needed as much experience and socialisation as possible. He might not be able to keep her, but his conscience insisted that he do the right thing by her, and if that meant taking her for a carry in the park on a lovely sunny evening, then that's what he would do.

First, though, photos.

Crikey, the pup was photogenic, he saw after he'd taken a few snaps. With each shot he took of her, she seemed to pose more and more, until he'd captured her with an assortment of expressions on her pretty face (if anyone had tried to tell him before now that dogs had expressions, he'd have thought they were mad), and in a variety of poses. And in every single image, she looked so darned cute it made his heart ache.

After a bit of a play, Poppy settled down in his lap as he switched his computer on and navigated his way around Gumtree. Should he give her away, or sell her, he wondered. Giving her away might attract the wrong sort of people, but on the other hand, selling her felt far too wrong. In the end, he decided on the words, "price negotiable, good home essential", and he'd see what came of it. Not having a definite price on Poppy's head might put some people off because they'd be worried they might not be able to afford her, but he hoped that one or two potential buyers would read between the lines and realise that the good home part would dictate the asking price.

It didn't take long to place an advert. The whole process was extremely easy. Too easy, maybe? For some reason, he felt it should be harder to buy and sell a dog like Poppy. She wasn't a Kenwood food mixer, or a used car – she was a living, breathing, loving animal. Therefore, it was up to him to screen potential buyers very carefully. He wasn't prepared to hand her over to just anyone; he had to be certain she was going to a doting caring home.

With a deep sigh and cursing his mother with every cell in his body, he gathered Poppy up and clambered to his feet. 'Right, little one, let's go for that walk. Although, you won't be able to walk on your own paws, you understand, because I've got to carry you for the rest of this week, but a bit of fresh air will be nice, won't it?'

Poppy licked the tip of his nose.

'Ew! You must stop doing that,' he said, chuckling despite his protests.

He found himself talking to her almost continually as he made his way out of the house and along the lane. The cottage he lived in was on the outskirts of

Pershore – a pretty little market town in the West Midlands – and just near enough so he could walk into town yet far enough away that he felt quite secluded. As a place to live, Pershore had everything he needed. More or less. It was sadly lacking in nightlife (but then, who'd want a raucous nightclub or a trendy bar on one's doorstep, he reasoned), but he could go into Worcester if he felt the need.

There was a lively high street filled with all kinds of quirky, artisan shops, a decent number of pubs, a couple of cafes, the odd restaurant, and a large landscaped park which he hadn't visited since he was a kid.

From what he remembered of it, there had been a bowling green (strictly out-of-bounds), swings, a slide and a roundabout (definitely within bounds), a bandstand (which had always smelt a bit strange) and flowerbeds with paths winding through them. There had also been a decent-sized field with a football pitch marked out complete with a couple of goalposts, that he'd never seen anyone actually play a game of footie on.

It hadn't changed much, he saw, as he strolled through the gates. There were possibly a few less people around than he remembered, especially little children; but kids today had more to occupy them indoors and he supposed that it might be suppertime for the littler ones.

There were some older kids, he noticed, who seemed to be occupied well enough by alcohol and cigarettes and were loitering noisily around the bandstand. The place hadn't changed a great deal at all, he decided, as he headed off in the opposite direction, not wanting to risk spotting any of his pupils engaging in under-age drinking. Or worse.

He was pleased to see there were other dog walkers around, although no one else appeared to be taking their pooch for a carry, and he did attract a few odd looks. But only until they noticed just how young Poppy was, then a glimmer of understanding flitted across their faces. Not one of the doggy people he passed could resist coming up to him for a closer look, and a stroke or two. Of the dog, not Theo obviously; although attention from a couple of women had been quite welcome. One of them, a twenty-something with a greyhound on a lead was very attractive indeed. And she gave him a lovely smile, one that he felt all the way down to his toes.

'Is that you, Poppy?' he heard a voice call, and Theo glanced around to see a familiar face.

'Hi, I didn't expect to see you here,' he said, noticing that Josie had three dogs with her. One of them was a Springer spaniel which he assumed was her own. The other two were breeds he didn't recognise. He'd only known what the greyhound was because he'd attended the dog races once.

'How was she when you got home from work?' Josie asked, her attention on Poppy.

'All over me. She wouldn't leave me alone for five minutes, so I thought I'd bring her out for a bit of fresh air.'

'She was as good as gold when I popped in,' Josie said. 'She's such a sweetie. It's a pity she couldn't have a run-around with Crumble. That would wear her out.'

He remembered Crumble was the name of her dog, and when the spaniel heard it mentioned, his already-wagging tail wagged even more furiously.

'If you've still got her next weekend, we should arrange to meet up,' she said.

Theo raised a mental eyebrow. Wow, this pup was making dating a doddle. Maybe he'd hang on to her for a bit longer?

It was only when he glanced at Josie's face that he realised she really did mean meeting up because it would be beneficial for the pup, and not for any other purpose. There wasn't a hint of flirting in her expression, and for some reason the lack of it sent a wave of disappointment through him.

Typical, he thought – he'd had more women flirting with him these past few days than he'd had for the whole of his life previously, and here he was feeling put out because Josie wasn't. Talk about wanting what you can't have, he mused. Just because she'd made no indication that she was interested in him, he felt all the more attracted to her. Which was ridiculous considering he knew absolutely nothing about her. She might be in a relationship for all he knew, and although he'd not seen any indication of a partner in her life when he'd checked her out on social media, it didn't mean to say there wasn't one.

Besides, the odds of him still having Poppy by next weekend were slim.

'Good idea,' he replied, his tone non-committal.

'Right, I'd best get on – I've got two more miles to walk with this lot before we're done.' She indicated the three dogs waiting patiently at her feet, her expression softening.

She certainly was nuts about dogs, wasn't she? Which was a good thing as far as he was concerned, because he knew the pup was in good hands when Josie was looking after her.

She gave him a friendly smile, and once again he thought how pretty she was, with her make-up free face (as far as he could tell), glowing complexion, glossy hair and clear, bright eyes. Then he had to bite back a chuckle as he realised he was practically describing her in pooch terms. He'd be saying she had a cold wet nose next!

Just as she was about to carry on with her walk, she placed a hand on his arm, the one that was holding Poppy, and said, 'You've got my phone number – let me know when you don't need me anymore; otherwise, I'll be in tomorrow to see to this little one.'

Her hand moved from his arm to the pup's head, and he wished she'd move it back. Her touch had been warm, and it had made his skin tingle. And she was close enough for him to smell the same delicious perfume that had been on Poppy's fur earlier. For some reason, it made his heart beat that little bit faster.

'Great. Thanks. See you tomorrow,' he blurted. 'Not that I'll be there, of course. I mean... Oh, you know what I mean.'

Josie was biting her lip, amusement flashing in her eyes. 'I do know what you mean. Bye, Theo. Bye, Poppy.'

The puppy was given a tickle under her chin. Theo was given another smile. He decided that Poppy had the better deal.

CHAPTER 9

Theo had no idea why the email in his inbox had come as such a shock to him. He'd already guessed that a cute young dog like Poppy would garner quite a lot of interest, so he had trouble understanding his reaction when he saw it on returning from the walk (carry, in the dog's case) later that evening.

And there was another one, and another, he saw, scrolling down. According to the time on the email, the first one had come in less than fifteen minutes after the advert had gone live.

He read it. Then he frowned.

The man who'd sent it hadn't said outright that he wanted a bitch for breeding purposes, but Theo could read between the lines. The guy already had a male and a female Cockapoo and he was asking lots of questions about Poppy's parentage, none of which Theo could answer, having not seen them himself. Besides, he didn't know what the difference was between a Toy poodle and a Miniature one, and he didn't care. And what was all this F1 and F2 malarkey?

He did a quick search, and the gut feeling that the guy was a breeder intensified when he read that F1 and F2 referred to whether a Cockapoo was a first- or second-generation crossbreed. If the bloke wanted her for a pet and had a loving home "ready and waiting" as he claimed in his email, he probably wouldn't care what generation Poppy was. There was no way Theo was going to let her go to a breeder. She deserved to be loved and cherished, not used as a puppy-making machine.

Theo deleted it and read the next email.

At first glance it sounded more promising, but when he got to the bit that said the couple had just had a new baby and wanted the child and the puppy to grow up together, he dismissed it. Did these people not realise how much work went into owning a dog? He'd only had Poppy for three days, and he was already exhausted. And not solely due to lack of sleep, either. He hadn't been able to take his eyes off her for a second in case she chewed something she wasn't supposed to or had a little accident behind the sofa. He had visions of Poppy being more and more ignored as the novelty of having a cute pup in the house wore off, and the reality of trying to look after a young baby and a boisterous adult dog kicked in.

Another no, then.

Ah, this one sounded good. The woman who'd sent this email already had one dog and wanted a companion for him as her other dog had recently died and the surviving one was mourning the loss.

Aww, that was so sad. Until now the thought that dogs could feel grief had never entered his head.

She was a definite possibility, but he wanted to make sure that the dog she already owned would get on with the new one, and as Poppy wasn't allowed to meet any other dogs until the weekend, he decided to hold fire on sending her a reply. Anyway, he wanted to see what other responses he got – he wasn't going to hand Poppy over to just anyone.

In fact, he was becoming alarmingly reluctant to hand her over at all!

CHAPTER 10

Thank God it was finally Friday! Theo closed the door to his classroom with a satisfying bang, and sped off along the corridor, freedom beckoning. The head teacher had wanted all the staff to meet for a few minutes after school in the hall so he could make a speech about how well the term had gone, and how he hoped everyone would have a restful break so they could return in September invigorated and full of enthusiasm.

Theo knew what Mr Fitzpatrick was going to say because he'd said the same thing for the past five years.

Theo also knew that the longer serving, wiser staff would be out of the door like greyhounds out of the trap, eager to begin six blessed weeks of no school. He was among the early escapees, and he headed for his car with an alacrity that bordered on training for the 100m in the Olympics.

He could see other staff members also scattering towards their vehicles or piling into the school minibus for the traditional end-of-academic-year piss-up in Worcester.

For once he wasn't one of them.

He'd decided he'd better get home to the dog.

He told himself it was because he was worried that if she was left on her own for too long, she might become destructive. Even though, up to now, she'd shown no inclination to take his kitchen apart, he wasn't about to take any chances that the idea to chew on a cupboard door or two might not enter her pretty little head.

The real reason was that from today the seven days of enforced walkie restrictions were over. Poppy could officially go out for a walk without risking catching some horrid canine disease. And as it was such a lovely afternoon, he couldn't wait to take her to the park.

Ever since he'd carried her around the park on Monday, he could sense that the dog wanted to get down. To let her trot by his side and allow her to sniff to her heart's content would be a joyful thing he decided, as he ducked down in the driver's seat. No way on earth was he about to let himself be accosted by Sable Smith's mum – not now that the school had officially closed its doors for the summer break. Sable and her mum would wait until September.

He doubted that it would be anything important (it never was) but Sable's mum seemed to think he had nothing better to do than to expect the school to find whatever her daughter had managed to lose that day, or investigate a remark which another child had made which Sable didn't like, or to speak to the school cook because darling Sable didn't like having her peas touch her carrots on her dinner plate. The list was as endless as it was irritating.

He watched Sable and her mother march across the car park and head towards reception, where he knew for a fact that the two ladies who manned the desk would have been out of the door precisely five seconds after the bell had gone in order to avoid exactly the sort of encounter that Sable's mother intended to have.

Whenever the word "snowflake" was mentioned, Sable Smith's entitled and smug little face popped into his head. God help them all, but she was only in Year 7. The school had another four years of dealing with the parent to look forward to and he thanked the Lord they didn't have a Sixth Form, because it would only serve to extend the pain.

That was the last time he intended to think about work until results day towards the end of August, he decided as the irate pair stomped out of sight, and he swiftly started his car and sneaked out of the car park, only breathing a huge sigh of relief when he was beyond the school gates.

Freedom! He felt exactly the same as he used to feel when he was a boy and the last day of school had ended and there were six long and wonderful weeks ahead of him filled with possibility and excitement. He supposed that was one good thing about teaching – that feeling never went away.

He'd have a takeaway again tonight he decided, because he'd never got to eat the Singapore vermicelli rice noodles he'd ordered last week, and then he paused as a thought hit him. He'd had Poppy one whole week.

It seemed much longer than that.

Much longer indeed.

Another thought occurred to him – now that she could mingle with other dogs, she'd be able to go for a walk with Josie's dog, Crumble.

A third thought popped into his head, which made him pause for far longer than the last one; so much so that he pulled over and reached for his phone.

Poppy would be able to meet that woman's dog, the woman who had emailed him via Gumtree, the one who wanted Poppy as a companion for her remaining pet.

Theo had received many more emails, some of which he'd instantly dismissed and some of which he was keeping on the back burner in case the woman with the deceased dog didn't work out, but he'd not yet responded to any of them.

The past seven days had flown by and it came as a bit of a shock to realise that this time last week he was unknowingly about to have a dog dumped on him. A dog who had spent the last one hundred and sixty-six hours busily worming her way into his heart.

If he didn't want one week to morph into two, then three, he'd have to do something about it.

Besides, she was cramping his style. If it wasn't for the dog, he'd be off out with the others in the minibus this afternoon, heading for the bright lights of Worcester and one of its three nightclubs. Or had one of them closed and it was now down to a choice of two?

Never mind; he was forgoing getting drunk because a small fluffy animal needed him at home. He'd not miss anything significant by not going to the end of term bash just this once. Although Robyn did say she was going, and she'd made her interest in him fairly clear. He hoped. Or had he imagined it? She certainly asked after Poppy every day when they met in the staffroom. And she'd mentioned more than once that she was single. If that wasn't showing an interest in him, then he didn't know what was. They'd even gone as far as to swap phone numbers, with the promise of meeting up in the summer hols. To do what, he had no idea. A drink? Or dinner?

It would be nice.

Robyn was nice.

It was also a relief that with Mr Donald's return in September, Theo wouldn't have the risk of running into her in the photocopying room if they did start seeing each other and things subsequently went belly-up. How awkward would that be? He'd seen it happen too often to count, and work was horrid enough already without adding bumping into an ex-girlfriend during assembly or at a staff meeting into the equation.

So, yeah, he might just give her a call…

First though, he needed to see whether the woman who wanted a companion for her pooch was still interested in Poppy.

She was, and he arranged for her to come around later that evening and bring her Tibetan terrier, Tinker, with her.

As he opened the kitchen door and a ball of fluff launched herself at him, Theo deliberately turned his mind away from the possibility that this might be the last time he was welcomed so enthusiastically and so joyfully in his own home. He crouched down to the dog's level and tried to prevent her from licking half of his face off in her delight at seeing him.

When she'd eventually calmed down and he'd mopped up the inevitable accidents, he changed into casual clothes and took her lead from the hook near the front door. Poppy, knowing what this meant, launched herself at him again, expecting to be picked up and carried outside.

Clipping her lead onto her little collar for what might be the final time, a pang of sadness pierced his chest. He'd had her for a week, just seven days, and she'd already lodged herself firmly in his heart. Despite her potential new owner arriving in an hour, it seemed only fitting that he was the one to take her on her first proper walk, and he was so glad he'd chosen to sacrifice a night out for these last few precious moments with the pup.

Mind you, the practical side of him chirped up, if he had decided to go on a bender and celebrate the end of the academic year in a fitting manner, then he wouldn't have arranged for a potential buyer to see the dog tonight; so he told himself to stop being so ridiculously maudlin and take the damned thing out.

Heeding his own advice, he headed towards the door, but he was pulled up short before he reached it, and when he looked behind him he saw Poppy sitting on her fuzzy little bottom, refusing to move.

A tug on the lead had her pulling backwards, her whole body tensing, and he realised she had no idea what was going on. One minute she was anticipating being carried, the next she was being dragged across the parquet floor towards the great outdoors.

He had to smile. She looked so indignant.

Relenting, he picked her up. It was probably a bit much to expect her to walk to the park and back. She was still only a baby, and her muscles and stamina hadn't properly developed yet. With that in mind, he carried her down the lane. He'd put her on the ground when they reached the park gates. Sooner if she started to wriggle.

Poppy hung in his arms, her paws flopping, content to gaze around her. Her nose twitched constantly, and her droopy ears were as pricked as they could be. She was certainly interested in what was going on and her head turned frequently at anything that caught her eye.

As always, she attracted the usual amount of attention, and Theo was forced to stop often as various people wanted to fuss and pet the dog. The majority of them were female.

He'd miss this, he thought, although he wouldn't miss having to clean up the little presents she left for him. Though to be fair, she had more or less got the hang of pooping outside. It helped that he made sure she went into the garden after she'd eaten, but she'd yet to master the art of not weeing on her puppy pads. At least she went on those and not the living room rug, he mused, and he guessed it wouldn't be long before she was properly house-trained.

They'd come a long way in those seven days. And she was sleeping most of the night, too. He distinctly remembered the morning of the first night that she hadn't woken him up with her howling and whimpering, and he'd rushed downstairs to check she was all right, relief making him feel sick when he realised she was perfectly fine.

Since then, having a young dog in the house had become considerably easier, although she still wasn't keen on letting him stay in bed much after six a.m. But that was OK – as long as he had seven hours unbroken sleep, he could cope, and he was no longer walking around like a zombie.

Reaching the entrance to the park, Theo placed the puppy gently on the path. She stood there, her paws rooted to the tarmac, sniffing frantically, her eyes wide as she tried to digest this new turn of events.

He spied a couple of other walkers with their dogs in the distance, but they were far enough away not to concern him for the moment. However, if they came any nearer and he was at all worried, he'd pick Poppy up; he didn't want her first encounter with another dog to be a negative experience.

Slowly, and with a great deal of encouragement, he persuaded the little pup to move, first one paw, then another, and another, until she was trotting along behind him. Sort of. Maybe dancing or cavorting would better describe her antics on the end of a leash. He wasn't sure whether she was protesting against being walked on the lead, or whether she was celebrating being able to use her own four paws at last.

Gradually she settled down, becoming far more interested in the assortment of interesting smells lining the grassy edges of the path than the fact that she was tethered to her owner by a length of leather, and Theo began to relax and enjoy himself. It was quite therapeutic strolling through the park on a summer's evening, but if he'd have attempted this on his own without a dog by his side, he'd have felt a bit of an idiot. Hiking up a mountain on one's own was one thing, but going out for a random stroll in the park on your tod, was bordering on being slightly strange, especially when the place often had a dozen or so Robert Crouch High School pupils hanging around.

A nudge on his calf made him look down.

Poppy was trotting just behind him, her nose on his leg and every so often she was trying to jump up and swiping him with her chunky paws.

He knew exactly what she wanted – she wanted to be picked up and carried, and he was about to give in to her demand when he spotted another dog out of the corner of his eye.

He recognised it at once as being Crumble, Josie's spaniel, and was pleased to see Josie herself following closely behind.

'She's walking by herself!' Josie exclaimed and Theo felt a rush of pride at the pup's accomplishment. 'Be gentle,' she warned her dog, and Crumble stood still to let Poppy approach him in her own time.

'He's very well behaved, isn't he,' Theo said, watching the two animals closely. Crumble's attention was on the puppy, and his tail was wagging so hard and fast it had become a blur, but he hadn't moved, despite his interest.

Poppy, on the other hand, didn't know how to react. One second she was bouncing around with her tail in the air, the next she was hiding behind Theo's legs with her tail curled under her tummy. She plainly had no idea what to make of this strange creature.

'I should hope so,' Josie laughed. 'I've spent hours and hours training him. But even now he can still forget himself on occasion. He's brilliant with other dogs though, and he adores puppies.'

Crumble, as though to show the truth of his mistress's statement, flicked out a long pink tongue and swiped Poppy across the nose with it. Poppy sneezed and Theo laughed, Josie joining in.

'Thank you for taking care of her while I was in work,' Theo said, his attention now on the carer. She was dressed in a pretty summery top and a pair of shorts which showed off her long, tanned legs. Her hair was tied back in a ponytail and she looked fresh-faced and natural. She also looked relaxed and happy – he hoped he was looking the same now that school was out for six glorious weeks.

'No problem. She's a sweetie. Anytime you need me to see to her you know where I am.'

'Er, I might not have to bother you again,' he said sheepishly, not wanting to admit that he had probably found Poppy a new home. It wasn't anything to be ashamed of; it wasn't as though he'd actively searched for a dog, bought one, then decided he didn't want it. Poppy had been thrust upon him without warning, and he was trying to do the responsible thing. So why was he feeling so shitty about it? 'I've, erm, got someone coming to have a look at her.' He checked the time. 'In about half an hour, to be exact, so I'd better get going.'

Josie's expression was inscrutable, but he had a feeling he was being judged and found sadly wanting. It wasn't a pleasant experience.

'It was nice to have met you, and I wish you all the best with the dog walking thing,' he said awkwardly.

'Nice to have met you, too,' she replied, and bent down to give Poppy a final ruffle of her ears. 'Be good for your new family; I'm sure you will be because you're such a cutie.'

And with that, Josie turned away after throwing a small smile in his direction.

Theo and Poppy watched the pair of them go for longer than was strictly necessary, before beginning their own journey back to the cottage and the start of a new life apart.

CHAPTER 11

'I'm Martha and this little tinker is Tinker!' the woman trilled; she had undoubtedly used the same introduction before, and Theo dutifully laughed.

'Ha ha, yes, well, hello Martha, and hello Tinker,' Theo said, scrutinising Poppy's potential new owner.

She was in her fifties; the dog's age was indeterminable. She was dressed up to the nines with high court shoes and one of the largest handbags Theo had ever clapped eyes on. The dog's coat was long and silky, and he wore a blue bow in the fur on the top of his head to keep it out of his eyes. She was smiling widely down at Poppy. Her dog, however, didn't look as enthusiastic about the new addition to the household. Not if his bared teeth and low warning growls were anything to go by.

Poppy hung back, keeping Theo's legs between her and the strangers, which didn't bode well for a happy rehoming.

Maybe she just needed time to become used to Martha and Tinker? It was bound to be strange for her. The only other person to have entered the house while she'd been living there, was Josie. And the only other dog she'd been close to was Crumble.

Now she was expected to welcome a strange woman and a slightly cross dog into the house she undoubtedly considered to be her own territory.

'Come in,' Theo said, scooping Poppy up and stepping aside to let Martha and her dog pass.

'Ooh, she's adorable! My friends will love her to bits, and they're all going to want one just like her!' Martha exclaimed, shoving her face at Poppy until she was only inches away, and making loud kissy noises.

Poppy recoiled and looked up at Theo anxiously.

'It's OK, Poppy-poppet,' he murmured absently. 'Go through into the living room,' he said to Martha, 'and the dogs can get acquainted. Your other one died, you said?'

'Yes, my little Benjie was cruelly taken from us a couple of months ago. Tinker misses him terribly and I was hoping he'd come to terms with it, but he hasn't yet, so I thought of getting him a little companion.' She sniffed rather theatrically.

Aw, poor Tinker, and poor you,' Theo said. Before Poppy had come into his life, he would never have considered how awful it was to lose a pet, but now any thought of something happening to her caused a lump in his throat. He could totally understand how Martha must be feeling. 'Had he been ill?'

'Car accident.'

'Oh, no, that's awful. Were either you or Tinker injured?' He put Poppy down, only to have her cower against his legs.

Tinker took a jerky step forward and bared his teeth. Poppy whimpered and scrabbled at Theo's knees, asking to be picked up again. When Tinker began to bark at her, the pup cried even louder. Theo picked her up, feeling her trembling against him.

'Not really,' Martha replied. 'It wasn't that sort of car accident. Benjie was run over.' She dabbed at the corner of one eye with the pad of her middle finger and sniffed. 'He escaped from my sister's garden. She always looks after my babies when I go away.'

Theo blinked. Clearly this unknown sister didn't do a very good job. 'Do you go away often?' he asked, feeling as if he was interviewing the woman for a job.

'A few times each year. I love my holidays in the sun. I usually go for a couple of months in the winter.'

He could tell; her skin was deeply tanned and slightly leathery looking. He'd thought it was from the lovely summer they were having, but the colour was probably too deeply ingrained to have been gained from a few weeks of British sunshine.

'Oh, where do you go?' He wasn't interested, but thought he'd better ask. Anything to fill the time until he could reasonably ask her to leave, as he'd already made his mind up that he wasn't going to let such a sweet-natured, trusting, loving little girl like Poppy go to a home where one dog had already been lost through carelessness. Or one where the owner would leave her charges for weeks at a time.

'Benidorm in the winter, and anywhere I can get a cheap flight to for the rest of the year,' she said airily. 'Now, let's get down to business. How much do you want for her? You said the price was negotiable, so let's negotiate!'

'I... um... er...' He was about to say he'd changed his mind, but he wasn't sure of her reaction, so instead he blurted, 'I've got other people coming to see her.'

'So?' Martha glared at him. 'I was here first and I've got the cash on me.'

'Yes, but I don't think Tinker and Poppy have hit it off, do you?'

Tinker's glare matched his owner's and Poppy squirmed uneasily on Theo's lap.

'They'll be fine.' Martha waved a hand in the air. 'His bark is much worse than his bite, and puppies that age need to learn manners. He's bound to boss her around.'

'No, he's not,' Theo said. 'I don't want her bossed by anyone, so I don't think I'll be letting her go to you. Sorry.' He got to his feet, making sure he had a good grip on Poppy.

'Well, I never!' Martha rose and huffed at him. 'You're nothing but a time-waster. Thanks for nothing!' And with that she stomped out of the living room on her high heels, dragging a still-growling Tinker behind her. She yanked the front door open and marched down the path, Tinker's long fur bouncing up and down as he trotted after her.

Theo waited until she'd climbed into her car before he closed the door and leant against it with a sigh of relief.

'She definitely wasn't right for you was she, my little one?' Poppy licked his ear, making him chuckle. 'I'll find you a really good home, I promise.'

Half-heartedly, he checked his emails again, reading the other responses his advert had generated.

Ah, maybe this one? A mum and dad with two children aged nine and twelve. They said they'd been wanting a dog for ages but had decided to wait until the children were old enough to understand what owning a dog meant. They sounded perfect, on paper at least. Although, he was a little concerned that they might not have owned a dog before and would therefore have no idea what they were letting themselves in for.

Just like him.

He'd have to make sure she wouldn't be left on her own all day, and that they realised just how hard work having a dog could be.

The mum sounded lovely on the phone, however – happy and excited that he'd called – and they could come straight over, if that was convenient for him?

It was.

Actually, it wasn't, because he was still reeling from Martha's visit, but he knew he had to let Poppy go at some point, and sooner would be far better than later for all concerned. Even though the thought of handing her over and watching her leave in another person's arms left a bad taste in his mouth, it had to be done.

He waited anxiously for the next potential new owners to arrive, Poppy curled on the sofa next to him, her head on his leg, her paws twitching as she slept, and he breathed in the sweet puppy scent of her for the last time. As he sat there, he tried to memorise the shape of her nose, how soft her fur felt under his fingers and the solid warmth of her little body cuddled against him.

A lump rose in his throat and he swallowed it back down. Crossly, he brushed a stray tear from his cheek, becoming angry with himself for being so silly.

One short week, that's all he'd owned her for. And he'd known from the start that he wasn't going to keep her. So why was he being so ridiculous?

The doorbell brought him out of his reverie, and he hurried to answer it.

The family waiting on the step was exactly what he had envisaged when the idea of finding Poppy a new home occurred to him. The children's faces lit up with excitement when they saw the puppy, but they made no move to approach her, instead waiting for her to go towards them.

One of them, the youngest, sat on the floor with his hand outstretched, and looked to his father for confirmation that he was doing the right thing.

'That's it, Jack, let her come to you and sniff you,' the child's dad said. 'You have to win a dog's trust and you don't want to scare her.'

'Have you had a dog before?' Theo asked.

'My wife and I both owned dogs when we were kids, but not since. And as a family only now do we feel that this is the right time. The children are old enough to appreciate a pet, and they're also old enough to help take care of one. This will be very much a family affair,' he said, 'and it's not a decision we've taken lightly.'

'I can see that,' Theo said, watching the way the children interacted with Poppy. The pair of them were outwardly calm, despite their obvious excitement, and were trying not to overwhelm the pup.

'You didn't say in the advert why you are selling her,' the mum queried.

'Ah, um, I didn't want a dog. My mother bought her without even asking me. Plus I work, so it's not fair to leave her on her own when I'm at school all day.'

'You're a teacher?'

'Yeah, maths.'

'Which school?'

'Robert Crouch.'

'Henry here goes to Spetchly Wood.'

'Good school,' Theo said.

'He loves it, and you're good at maths, aren't you Henry?' the boy's mother said, and the child nodded.

'It's my favourite subject. I like textiles, too, but I can't do that next year because I have to do food technology,' Henry replied.

Theo smiled. The lad was articulate and confident, and he wished the boy was in his class. He could definitely do with a few more Henrys to balance things out.

'At least you would be home with her in the holidays,' Henry's mum pointed out. 'It's a pity you have to let her go – she seems such a sweet little thing.'

'Oh, she is,' Theo gushed. 'She's so loving; she follows me from room to room, and I had a devil of a job to get her settled at night. She's fine now,' he added hastily, in case they thought the dog was going to keep everyone awake for weeks. 'I'm sure she'll soon get used to you and her new routine. She's getting the hang of toilet training, and she's been out for her first proper walk today on her own paws. She can be a bit shy, though, and you'll have to take it slowly when introducing her to new things and new situations…' He trailed off and bit his lip, blinking hard.

He knew he was going to let her go this evening; Poppy would have a good home with these people, he felt. The stab of regret and sadness that the dog would be spending the last few minutes under his roof, took him by surprise. He knew she would be well cared for, and would be treated as one of the family. They'd love her just as much as he did—

Wait now, what was that?

Nah, he didn't love Poppy. He cared for her (who wouldn't?) but he hadn't given his heart to her. It simply wasn't possible to fall in love with a dog in the space of seven days. To the hour. To the minute, in fact. At precisely this time last week, his mother had dumped a frightened little puppy in his arms and informed him that it belonged to him.

He was willing to concede that giving Poppy away would leave a hole in his heart, but he had to weigh that up against going to the pub with his mates whenever he wanted, as well as having to make sure someone looked after her when he was at work (at that moment Josie's face popped into his head and his insides did a funny little lurch). He'd be able to sleep in past six in the morning, too.

On the other hand, he didn't go to the pub all that often; the pup would soon grow into an adult dog and wouldn't expect to get up at silly o'clock; and he could always ask Josie if walking Poppy on every school day could be a permanent arrangement. Yes, it would cost him, but he didn't spend much money on anything else. He hardly went on hols since all his mates had acquired other halves, he didn't have a mortgage to pay since Granny had left him her cottage, and he had no real interests or hobbies – he was either in work or watching Netflix. His could hardly be called an expensive or an extravagant lifestyle. Or a very interesting one, for that matter.

No wonder his mum thought he needed livening up a bit. She was right. He did. He wasn't sure having a dog would have been the way he would have chosen to do the livening up, but Poppy was here now, in his house – and in his heart.

Could he let her go, knowing he'd probably never see her again?

He didn't think he could.

In fact, he was certain he couldn't.

'Um, kids, go outside with your father for a moment, will you?' the woman said.

'Huh?' Both Theo and the children's father turned to the mum, and all three wore similarly surprised expressions.

The two boys were a credit to their upbringing, because they didn't argue or complain; they merely got to their feet and waited for their father to take them outside. The dad shot his wife a questioning look, but she merely shooed him away with a wave of her fingers.

She waited until they'd gone before she turned to Theo and said, 'I know this is none of my business and I'd dearly love to take the puppy home with us today, but I don't think you really want to let her go, do you?'

No, he didn't.

'And I think she's perfectly happy here,' the woman added, nodding her head at Poppy, who was busily licking his fingers and wagging her tail. 'Don't do anything rash. My advice would be to take your time and seriously think about it, because I don't believe you want to rehome her, and I think you'll seriously regret it if you do.'

'But what about—?'

'Leave the boys to me. They're sensible children, and they'll want to do the right thing.'

'Is it the right thing?' Theo asked, cuddling Poppy to him.

'Only you know that, but from where I'm sitting, I think it is.' She got to her feet, and Theo scrambled to his.

'Have a think. If you still believe it's the right decision to let the puppy go, give me a call.' She laid a hand on his arm. 'She'll have a good home with us, but I also think she'll have a good home with you.'

Theo gulped and nodded. 'Thank you,' he managed as he saw her to the door. 'I'll probably be in touch.'

She smiled at him, her expression kind. 'Somehow, I doubt that,' she said, then she was gone, leaving Theo clutching a bewildered little dog.

What was he supposed to do now?

Keep her? Call the Johnson family back?

He had no idea what he should do. So he called Josie.

It was the only thing he could think of.

CHAPTER 12

'I've got an idea,' Josie said after listening to his rather incoherent story a few minutes later. 'I'll have her at my house for the weekend, and see how you get on without her. If you don't miss her, then you're doing the right thing to give her away. If you pine for her, then you need to have a serious rethink about whether you should keep her or not.'

It was a good suggestion, a logical one. But he wasn't sure he was entirely comfortable with it. He didn't like to push the poor dog from pillar to post just because he couldn't make his mind up about what he wanted. It wasn't in the dog's best interest to stay with Josie, then come back to his, before maybe going to live somewhere else. Being so unsettled could scar the pup for life.

When he said as much, a deep sigh drifted on the airways. 'Have you got a better plan? Because you don't seem to. For her sake, you need to make a decision.'

Josie was right; he did.

'Do you want to come and get her, or should I bring her to you?' he asked.

'I'll fetch her. I could do with getting out of this house for a while.'

'Oh, sorry, I didn't… Will having Poppy cause any problems? With your other half, I mean? Although, in your profession, I suppose he's used to you doing the occasional spot of dog boarding.'

'I don't have a other half, so that's not an issue. I need to get out of the house because I'm having my kitchen refitted and the mess is getting to me. Especially since the builder has disconnected my oven and hob, the sink is leaking, which means I can't cook anything.'

'Come to mine.'

'I said I'd fetch Poppy.' She sounded short-tempered.

'I meant, come to mine for some dinner. I've got chicken that needs to be used up, and I can't eat it all myself. I was thinking of enchiladas.' He had an Old El Paso kit in the cupboard, he recalled. He wasn't sure how long it had been there, but those things never went off, right? Also, he had no idea how those words had come out of his mouth or why, but now that they had he prayed she'd say yes. Poppy was good company an' all, but she wasn't exactly hot on the conversational front.

The pause went on for so long that Theo wondered if they'd been cut off. Or if she'd hung up on him… 'Hello?'

'Yes, I'm still here. Enchiladas would be nice; thank you for inviting me.'

'And bring Crumble, too,' he added, feeling generous.

'I was going to,' came the short reply.

And so she did, turning up at his door less than three-quarters of an hour later, complete with a bottle of wine and a waggy-tailed spaniel. 'I was going to drink it in lieu of supper,' she stated, holding up the wine, 'so I thought we could share.'

'Great idea. Come on in.'

She handed him the bottle and stooped to pet Poppy, who was dancing and jumping excitedly at her feet, while Crumble sniffed Poppy's ears and gave them a bit of a wash with his long tongue.

He gestured for her to walk ahead into the kitchen where the enchiladas were happily bubbling away in their cheesy tomato sauce, and all evidence of the box having been cleared away. He wasn't averse to taking the credit, although if she asked whether he'd cooked the dish from scratch, he'd be honest and let her think he was tidy instead.

'Hello, gorgeous,' she crooned to the puppy. 'You're coming to my house for a little visit. How about that? I'm going to spoil you rotten, just you wait and see.' She straightened up and turned her attention to him. 'I'll keep her from tonight until Monday morning. Will that give you enough time to decide?'

'I hope so.' His reply was earnest. 'Should we do this through *The Next Best Thing*?'

'Let's leave them out of it, shall we?'

'OK.' If Josie wanted to keep all the payment for herself and not have the organisation take their cut, then he didn't mind. 'How much do I owe you?'

'Nothing. I'm not doing this for the money. I'm doing it for Poppy. And for you.' The last was definitely an afterthought on her part, he realised, her tone tart.

'Right. Good. Well, then, shall we eat? I'm about to give Poppy her supper, too, so would Crumble like some? It's puppy food, but I feel mean feeding my dog without giving your dog something.'

He caught her quick smile at the words "my dog". She seemed to really want him to keep Poppy and, rather uncharitably, he wondered if it was purely for the business that he'd most likely send her way if he did.

Her whole expression had softened however, and he decided he didn't care about the reason. He liked seeing her smile. He liked seeing *her*, full stop.

Maybe, even if he did decide that Poppy would be better off with the Johnson family, he could suggest going out for a meal or a drink to Josie? He wasn't a bad bloke – she knew he had Poppy's best interests at heart. But was it him she was interested in, or just the dog?

'Ooh, this is lovely,' she exclaimed a short while later as they tucked into chicken enchiladas with a side salad, and some tortilla chips and salsa dip. It looked as though he'd made an effort and put some thought into the meal, when in reality the chicken had been in the freezer for weeks, the enchilada kit had been in his cupboard for months, and the tortilla and dip combo was a staple part of watching a box set on a Friday evening, along with a couple of beers on occasion.

Tonight though, he was drinking wine and sharing his tortillas with Josie. And he was thoroughly enjoying himself.

'It's just a little something I threw together,' he said modestly, crossing his fingers in the hope that she wouldn't enquire too deeply into the spices he'd used because he couldn't recall what it had said on the box.

'Do you do much cooking? I know I don't – I usually can't be bothered to go to all that effort just for myself,' she said.

'I have been known to shove something in the oven

now and again.' His answer was evasive. He didn't want her to know he was more or less useless in the kitchen, and neither did he want to blow a trumpet he neither didn't own nor couldn't play.

'Good for you. I like a man who isn't scared of a kitchen.'

'Are there many men still like that these days?' he asked around a mouthful of salad. 'I mean, us men are far more enlightened than we used to be, and many of us live on our own so we have to be self-sufficient.' He was very self-sufficient at piercing the plastic films on microwaveable meals, and he was equally self-sufficient at ordering a takeaway. Every other Sunday, he showed how self-sufficient he could be by popping to his mum's for a roast lunch. Oh, yeah, he was self-sufficient all right...

She liked a man who wasn't scared of a kitchen, eh? All he hoped was that she wouldn't find out he was equally as scared of an ironing board, and he was slightly frightened of the vacuum cleaner. As for cleaning the windows, he was terrified!

These were all the things he knew he should be doing as a person who was solely responsible for the upkeep of his own house, but they were also the things he didn't think about doing unless his mum reminded him (the word was "nagged") or he had a visitor. And by "visitor" he was talking of someone of the opposite sex. His mates didn't notice stuff like grubby windows or dust bunnies behind the TV. And in the rare event that they did notice, they wouldn't care.

Josie would probably care though, which was why he'd taken pains to keep the cottage looking nice since his frantic cleaning session last week.

And if he was totally honest, Poppy was helping him keep the place clean and tidy – which was a revelation, considering he'd always assumed that owning a dog meant there were pet hairs and mud everywhere.

On the contrary, Cockapoos didn't shed (so he'd read) and the weather was too dry for mud. As for the rest of it, he was forced to keep the floors clean and debris free, because madam had a habit of stealing and trying to chew anything which she thought was fair game. Including his work shoes. He was also forced to mop the kitchen floor on a regular basis because of her little accidents. So that was a definite plus to owning a dog.

He gradually became aware that Josie was staring at him. 'Sorry, I was miles away for a second. Thinking about the dog,' he added, semi-truthfully.

'I understand. It must be hard for you.' She reached across the table and placed her small slim hand over his.

Theo froze as his skin tingled at her touch and his

heart missed a beat. Her hand was warm on his, her touch gentle. It sent goose bumps along his arm, and he shivered involuntarily.

Josie noticed and quickly withdrew her hand. Theo wanted to tell her it was OK and to ask her if she'd put it back, but he daren't. It would sound a bit needy and desperate, and maybe even a tad creepy.

He smiled widely at her instead, and offered her more wine. She nodded and he refilled her glass, careful not to pour too much in so that she got the impression he was trying to get her drunk.

Bloody hell, this dating thing was a minefield.

Not that they were on a date of course; but if they were…

Once again, he considered the possibility and decided he liked the idea. A lot. He'd ask her out. Not now, not with the Poppy situation up in the air. But soon, once everything was resolved one way or another.

Searching around for something to say that didn't make him sound like a complete knob, he said, 'What made you decide on caring for dogs as a career?'

'As opposed to caring properly for them and becoming a vet or a nurse?' she retorted, and he winced as he realised his innocent question had touched a nerve he wasn't aware existed.

'That's not what I meant,' he objected. 'I just

wondered, that's all…'

'Sorry, I'm a bit prickly about it. My parents can't understand why I threw away a perfectly good degree to pick up other people's dog poo for a living.'

'Gross.' Theo made a face.

'Yes, that's how they put it. And yes, cleaning up after a dog is part and parcel of the job. But it's only a tiny bit of it.' Her expression brightened. 'Unless you're talking about Goliath, the Great Dane, and then it's a very big part of it,' she joked.

'What's your degree in?'

She sighed. 'Economics and politics.'

'What did you originally want to do with it?'

'No idea. It sounded interesting, that's all.'

'And was it?'

'Not in the slightest. But I persevered and got a first, and then told my parents that I'd found a job. They were over the moon – until I told them what the job was.' Her expression was neutral, but Theo noticed the pain in her eyes. 'Anyway,' she continued, 'I love animals, dogs especially, and I have to walk my own, so why not combine it with walking other peoples' pooches and get paid for it at the same time?'

Why not indeed? 'You seem happy in your work,' he stated.

'I am. I love my job. It'll never make me rich, but I earn enough to pay the bills and put food on the table, and with a bit left over to save up for a new kitchen. It'll be nice when it's done,' she added. 'I hope.'

'I'm sure it will be.' Theo gathered up their plates and took them to the sink. 'Are you sure you're OK to have Poppy, considering the mess you must be in?'

'I'm sure. There's no real mess, as such. Just an empty space where my old units were. The builder is doing the job on the side, so he's fitting it in when he can. He should be back on Monday evening to fix the units in place. They're stacked in my garage at the moment, and the car has been relegated to the road outside my house.'

'If I can help in any way...? Do you want to pop around tomorrow evening? I could order a takeaway?' Even as the words left his lips, he realised how ridiculous the suggestion was; if she wanted a takeaway, she was perfectly capable of eating it in her own house – it didn't exactly require any cooking, did it?

'I'm good, thanks. I'm going to visit a friend tomorrow lunchtime, and she said she'll feed me. Then on Sunday my parents are taking me out to lunch. Don't worry, the dogs will come with me. I hardly ever go anywhere without Crumble, and if a pub doesn't accept dogs then I don't go there.'

'But what about Poppy? She can be a bit of a handful.'

Josie raised her eyebrows. 'I don't believe you. Look

at her.'

Theo looked. Poppy and Crumble were curled up together in Poppy's basket, both of them fast asleep. It was a bit of a squash, but neither dog appeared to mind.

They looked incredibly sweet together.

'She'll be fine, especially with Crumble showing her how to behave. That's how puppies learn best – from older dogs.'

'If you're sure…?' Theo said doubtfully. 'And I insist on paying you. I wouldn't dream of teaching for a couple of days and not being paid for it.'

Josie bit her lip. She was plainly tempted.

'I feel as though I'm taking advantage of you,' he continued.

'It was my suggestion that Poppy comes to stay with me.'

'You only suggested it to help me out,' Theo pointed out.

She carried on worrying at her lip with her teeth, and he couldn't help staring at her mouth. What would it feel like to kiss her—?

'OK, but not at the full rate,' she suggested.

'Huh? Oh, yes, great. That's settled then.' He cleared his throat to try to dispel the imagined feel of her lips on his. 'You tell me what I owe you, and we'll go from there. Dessert?'

She blinked at the sudden change of subject. 'Why not? What is it?'

That was a very good question. He didn't have so much as a square of chocolate in the house. But what he did have was cheese and biscuits. And honey. Honey didn't go off either, did it? He sliced the cheese, cut up an apple and drizzled a little honey in a wavy pattern on the side. Along with a plate of crackers, it looked quite professional. 'Sorry I don't have anything sweet and gooey with cream, but will this do?'

'It looks heavenly,' she said. 'What's this?' She pointed to the golden drizzle.

'Honey. Go on, dip a slice of cheese in it and take a bite.'

Josie did as he suggested, and he watched as she closed her eyes in delight and made yummy noises. Abruptly his imagination showed him an image of her lying on a pillow, with her eyes shut and those same noises—

'Crikey, that's good!' she exclaimed. 'I'd never have thought of putting cheese, apple and honey on the same plate before.'

'I'm glad you like it.'

'Like it? This is my new foody addiction.'

He hated to ask, but he couldn't help himself. 'What non-food addictions do you have?'

Josie paused, a sliver of apple oozing with delicious

honey halfway to her mouth. Slowly a flush spread across her cheeks. 'Not the kind of addictions you are referring to. I don't actually have any addictions that aren't food related. You could say I am addicted to walking, I suppose. Even though I have a car, I tend to walk whenever I can.'

Theo tended to drive. Even if it was to the nearest shop and back. 'Me too,' he said. 'I love walking.'

'That's another reason why you should think long and hard about rehoming Poppy. Considering you already enjoy walking, the great outdoors is a hundred times better with a dog. And it'll make you go out and get some exercise every day, even if you don't feel like it or the weather is foul.'

'You're not selling this dog-thing to me, you know,' he joked. 'Anyway, if I did decide I can't live without her, then I'll employ you to take her for a walk if it's hammering down with rain. There's no point in both of us getting wet.'

'There's no such thing as bad weather, only inappropriate clothing,' she replied primly. 'You ought to see me in my waterproof trousers and wellies.'

An image sprang into his head, and he couldn't shift it. The wellies featured quite prominently.

Gah! He was turning into a right idiot. What was wrong with him?

'Can I help with the washing up?' she asked, cutting

across his confused and rather disturbing thoughts.

'It's OK, I'll see to it.' He didn't want to spend precious time clearing up when he could spend it sitting in the living room with her and finish off the wine. Besides, it was still quite early, not even nine p.m., and the night was still young, as they say.

Josie stood up. 'Right then, as much as I hate to disturb the pair of them, I must be making tracks. I want to get Poppy settled in and used to my house before I go to bed.'

Of course she did. Theo felt bad that he hadn't given poor Poppy a thought for the last half hour – he'd been too focused on Josie. 'Good idea. I'll fetch her collar and lead, and some puppy food.'

It was odd seeing Poppy trotting behind Josie as she made her way down his path, Crumble hot on her heels. The three of them looked perfect together, and it gave him a bit of a pang to watch them leave.

And for some considerable time afterwards, he wasn't sure which of them the pang had been for.

Eventually, after finishing what was left in the bottle of wine and staring thoughtfully into space, he concluded that had been for both of the new ladies in his life. Crumble, not so much…

CHAPTER 13

Theo couldn't settle. The house felt too empty, and he was acutely aware of the lack of another warm body, even though that particular warm body slept in a basket in the kitchen.

He'd missed saying goodnight to the dog and giving her a final cuddle before tucking her in with her own special blanket. And he'd found himself sniffing the material because he missed her sweet puppy scent. It had been far too quiet too, despite having the TV on.

And now, lying in bed, he was unable to sleep for wondering how the little pup was faring. Was she missing him? Or was she perfectly happy in her temporary home?

He was tempted to give Josie a ring to ask, but it was late and she'd probably be in bed. And he didn't want to come across as a wimp. There was a fine line between caring and being pathetically needy. The morning would be soon enough to check on Poppy.

He kept telling himself that, but it didn't appear to be doing much good. He still desperately wanted to know if Poppy was OK, even though he knew she most assuredly was.

It had only been three hours.

Three unexpectedly long hours.

He was forced to admit that he was missing her. Badly.

He certainly hadn't been anticipating that, and it came as rather a shock. Missing a person? That was completely understandable. But missing a dog? Hmm…

It took him a long time to fall asleep, so he was cross with himself when he woke at the ridiculous time of six-twenty-five. When he realised it wasn't Poppy who had disturbed him, he led there for a while wondering what he was supposed to do with himself for the rest of the day.

Unable to get back to sleep, he rolled out of bed and trudged down the stairs. He'd feel better after a cup of coffee, but when he entered the kitchen and saw the empty basket, his eyes filled with tears.

Theo managed to wait until seven a.m. before he called Josie, secure in the knowledge that Poppy would have made sure she was awake, even if Crumble didn't do early mornings.

'It's me, Theo. How is she?'

'Good morning!' Josie sounded chirpy. 'She's fine; a bit subdued but that's to be expected, considering she's in new surroundings.'

'But she knows you, right?'

'She knows you better.'

'Ah. But she's OK?'

'She's fine,' Josie repeated.

'Do you think she's missing me?' Theo persisted.

'What do you want me to say? That she is? Will that make you feel any better? It's not about her – well, it *is*, but you know what I mean. She'll soon get used to being with new people and in a new place. She's young and she'll adapt. The question is, how do you feel about being apart from her? Relieved? Upset? Missing her?'

All of the above, Theo thought, but he wasn't quite prepared to admit it to anyone else but himself yet.

Then he heard her play-growl, the cute little noise she made deep in her throat when she was playing tug, and he knew that if he was holding her he'd be able to feel the rumble of her chest as she pretended she was all grown up and fearsome.

And it hit him – a sudden rush of love for the little scrap of fur he'd unwittingly and reluctantly become an owner of, and he knew in his heart that he couldn't let her go.

'Can I have her back?' he asked abruptly.

'Of course you can; I'm not going to keep her, you know.'

'I mean now. Right this minute. Can I come and get her?'

There was silence for a second, then Josie spoke. 'She'll be waiting for you.'

Theo rushed to get dressed, then dashed out of the house, eager to cuddle his little girl. He was so keen to hold her, that he was hot and breathless by the time he reached Josie's house.

She lived nearer to the town centre than he did, on a street lined with Victorian villas on one side and small terraced houses on the other. Josie lived in one of the terraced ones, with a little front garden and a bay window upstairs and down. It looked neat, tidy and well cared for.

She answered his knock and invited him in. Curious, he gazed around, noting the vintage tiled floor in the hall, the narrow flight of stairs, and the light and airy feel of the place despite its small size. The living room was just as bright and cheerful, but he had eyes only for his dog.

His dog. Poppy was his, and he was Poppy's and that's the way it was going to be from now on. He'd take her with him whenever and wherever he could, and when he was unable to, then he'd book Josie to take care of her.

The pup was chewing on Crumble's ear, and didn't notice him at first, despite the older dog thumping out a greeting with his tail. But when she glanced up and saw him, she let out a little whimper of acknowledgement and scampered across the room. Theo dropped to his knees and she leapt into his arms, smothering his face with excited sloppy kisses, wriggling frantically with joy. Theo bent his head and kissed her between the ears, trying to hold the squirming ball of fur still so he could have a proper cuddle; but she was far too happy to see him to stay still for more than a split second. Eventually though, she wore herself out, and her twisting and turning settled down and she contented herself with licking his fingers and uttering little cries of happiness.

Theo caught Josie's eye. She was perched on the arm of a squashy sofa watching him with a soft, almost dreamy expression on her face.

He hadn't decided to keep Poppy to gain his dog sitter's approval, but he was nevertheless pleased he had it. For some reason it was important that she didn't think badly of him.

Just then his phone rang and he wondered who on earth it could be at this time on a Saturday morning. He narrowed his eyes when he saw who it was. He took the call, sending Josie a silent apology with his eyes.

'Hi, Mum, did you have a good time in Harrogate?'

He still hadn't forgiven her completely for what she'd done, but he was half-way there. He just wished she'd consulted him first; but he was also realistic enough to know that if she'd had mentioned him having a dog he'd have blown the idea out of the water. And he would never have known the sheer joy that Poppy had brought into his life. And that would have been an awful shame.

'Lovely, thanks. How's Poppy?' His mother sounded cheerful and not in the slightest bit contrite or remorseful.

'She's fine, no thanks to you. I can't believe you dumped her on me and buggered off.'

'You coped, didn't you?'

'I didn't want to have to cope.' He caught Josie's eye again and pulled a face. 'My mum,' he mouthed.

'I gathered that,' she mouthed back, and they shared a smile.

'Are you out with the dog?' his mum asked. 'I rang the house phone and there was no answer.'

'I might have been asleep.'

'With a pup in the house?' She barked out a laugh.

'OK, yes, I'm out with the dog.'

'Who looked after her for you last week when you were in work?'

'What do you care? You did a drop and run manoeuvre, if you remember. You weren't so bothered then about who'd look after the poor little thing while I was in school'

'Yes, your father and I feel bad about that.'

He heard his dad's voice in the background, saying,' Leave me out of this. It was all your idea.'

Theo said, 'A lovely lady helped me out. Her name is Josie—'

'Poppy, no!' Josie cried as the pup, fed up with no longer being the centre of attention, leapt out of Theo's arms and widdled on the rug.

'Sorry,' Theo said to Josie. 'I didn't think. I should have guessed she'd need a wee. Hang on, Mum—'

'I've got it,' Josies said. 'She's not the first dog to have peed on my rug. You finish your call, and I'll take her outside to remind her that's where she needs to go potty.'

'Theo? Theo? Is Everything all right? Theo!' His mother was shouting down the phone.

'Everything's fine. Poppy had a little accident, that's all.'

'Is she OK? What kind of accident?'

'A weeing on a rug kind of accident.'

'I thought you said you were out? And who's voice did I hear?'

Theo rolled his eyes. His mum didn't miss a thing. 'I'm at Josie's house.'

'Josie as in the woman who you said helped you

out?'

'That's right.'

'How old is she?' his mother demanded.

'Thirty-one; not that it's any of your business.'

'A girl, you mean, not a woman. Someone your own age.'

'She's definitely a woman,' he retorted irked beyond measure. What was it with mums and their inability to keep their noses out of their grown-up children's business?

His mother's tone of voice became less indignant and more nosey. 'Is she pretty?'

'Yes, Mum, she's extremely pretty, but there's nothing going on.' He knew exactly what she was getting at.

'How can you say that when you're at her house at this time on a Saturday morning? Do you think I was born yesterday? I can't—'

'I'm hanging up now. Goodbye.' He ended the call to find Josie standing behind him with her arms folded and another of those hard to read expressions on her face.

Oh God, how much of the conversation had she heard?

Enough, he guessed, else why would she be staring at him like that? 'Er, that was my mother.'

'We've already established that.'

She… erm… got hold of the wrong end of the stick. About me being here, I mean. I'll set her straight when I see her next.' He took a deep breath. 'So, are you able to look after Poppy when term starts in September?'

'I don't see why not.'

'Good, good…' Crikey, this was awkward. 'How much do I owe you for last night?'

'The meal you cooked me covered my fee.'

'That's not what we agreed.'

'No, it isn't. We agreed for me to have Poppy until Monday. It's only Saturday.'

'I realise that, but I should still pay you for last night. In fact, I should pay you for the whole weekend.'

'There's no need. Besides, when I agreed to your terms, I knew you'd come and fetch her today.'

'You did?'

'I was 99 per cent certain,' she amended.

'You were? How? Why?'

'I can tell when someone has fallen in love with their dog. And you, sir, are in love with yours. You can no more give her up, than I could find a new home for Crumble.'

Crumble heard his name mentioned and his tail thumped the floor. Poppy wagged hers too, just because she had one to wag and not to be left out, Theo assumed.

He shrugged. Josie was right. 'Do you think you

could have her one day a week from now until I go back to work? I don't want it to be too much of a shock for her.' He was aware that he was sounding more like an anxious parent about to leave a young child in nursery for the first time than a dog owner, but he didn't care.

Josie cocked her head to the side. 'Good idea.'

He got the impression she was surprised at his suggestion. That she didn't think he had it in him to be so empathetic to the needs of a small dog.

'We can go for a couple of walks together, too,' she said. 'It'll get her used to the other dogs I look after on a regular basis.'

Theo tried not to let his dismay show. He really wanted Poppy to be her sole charge, so she could lavish all her attention on the pup, but he recognised he was being unrealistic.

'When should we go for our first one?' Theo asked.

'Pardon?'

'Out first walk, when do you suggest?'

'I meant Poppy, not you too.'

'Oh. OK. No problem. Ha ha. I'm sure I can find something exciting to do with the time.'

'I'm sure you can.'

There was a small silence, during which Theo realised he should collect his dog and return home – he'd taken up enough of Josie's time this morning.

'I'll be off then,' he said, and Josie fetched Poppy's lead and the bag of puppy food and went to hand them to him. 'You might as well keep that here,' he said, seeing the biscuits, and she nodded her agreement.

After a few more pleasantries and promises to sort things out with *The Next Best Thing*, Theo finally stepped out of Josie's front door and was on his way, Poppy trotting at his heel. He was acutely aware of Josie's gaze following him as he walked down the little path, and he grew warm, far warmer than the early summer morning warranted.

It was when he unlatched her gate and stepped through it, that she spoke again and took him totally off guard.

'Do you really think I'm pretty?' she called after him.

Theo blanched, stopped and turned slowly back to face her. She *had* heard. Bugger.

There was no point in lying or being evasive. So he told the truth.

'Yes, I do. Very pretty,' he said, and with that, he was off down the road as fast as Poppy's little legs could carry her, his cheeks warm and his heart even warmer.

CHAPTER 14

Six weeks should be long enough to house train a dog, right?

Theo was busy making plans, and the first item on his to-do list was to train the pup to go to the toilet in the garden. With this aim in mind, as soon as he returned from collecting Poppy from Josie's he rushed her straight out into the garden and waited somewhat impatiently for her to do what he wanted her to do.

Typically, she refused, no matter how often he told her to 'do a wee' (hoping none of his neighbours heard him) and typically, the second he looked away she squatted, as the little puddle on the patio testified.

He still gave her plenty of praise, even though he hadn't caught her in the act because he'd been too busy checking out the garden to keep an eye on her. The old cottage's garden had six-foot-high brick walls surrounding it, and a suitably high wooden gate on the side. There was no way the dog was getting through, under or over it, and he toyed with the idea of putting some kind of a cat (dog) flap in the back door, so she could come and go as she pleased. If it worked for cats, surely it must work for dogs? But with no idea how large she'd grow, he wasn't sure how feasible it would be, especially considering his back door was mostly all glass. It was great for letting the light in and for allowing Poppy to be able to see into the garden, but as for putting a doggy door in, he wasn't sure it would work. Anyway, it was a thought for another time, when she was older and fully grown.

Next on his list for today was breakfast – for him, not the dog as she'd already had hers – then he intended to make an appointment with a vet to get her checked over, and after that he'd find out if there were any puppy training classes nearby. He wanted her to come when she was called, and to sit and stay before he went back to work. Six weeks should be long enough for that too, shouldn't it?

After that, he intended to Poppy-proof the house. He'd already made a half-hearted attempt at placing anything dangerous and/or precious out of the reach of sharp little teeth, but he didn't want to be spending the next few months as she went through the teething stage having to watch her continually to ensure she didn't get up to any mischief.

As he glanced around with dog-conscious eyes, he decided that the camera in the kitchen could stay for the time being, so he could check what she was getting up to when he was out – and he intended to be out every single day. Not for long, only five minutes to start with, but he wanted to get her used to him not being there all the time, because the risk was that he'd spend every waking hour from now until the end of the school holidays with the dog and come September she'd have difficulty accepting that he had to go back to work.

'Start as you mean to go on,' he muttered, looking online for the nearest vet practice. Ooh, look, there was one in the high street. Result! And they were open this morning.

He gave them a call and was pleased to be told there was a slot available at eleven – plenty of time for Poppy to have a snooze and for him to finish his house-checking.

Mindful that she wouldn't settle of her own accord if he was pottering about, he put her in her basket, told her to go to sleep, and closed the kitchen door on her.

Then he checked his phone to see what she was getting up to.

Poppy stared at the door for a moment, her head on one side listening, and Theo held his breath hoping she wasn't able to hear him breathing through the door. After a minute or so, she stretched as she climbed out of her basket and strolled around the kitchen. So far, so good, he thought. Until, that is, she found a spot she liked and plonked her bottom down on it, and he watched her lift her chin, point her cute little nose at the ceiling, and emit a mournful howl.

Oh my God, it was sweet and funny and heart-breaking all at the same time. That such a little creature could make such a loud noise was impressive, and the song she sang was melodious for a few seconds, until it degenerated into a series of little yips.

He couldn't allow her to cry like that – the neighbours would complain for one thing, and for another it broke his heart to see her so desolate – so he pressed the speaker button on his phone and said a firm 'No' into it.

Poppy stopped yelping and cocked her head to the side as she looked at the camera, then her head tilted to the other side as she tried to make sense of why her master's voice was coming from a black box above the microwave. Oh God, she was simply gorgeous when she did that.

Theo waited a few moments, hoping that was the end of it, but she soon started up again. 'Whooo-hooo-wooooo,' she cried mournfully, and he stifled a laugh. She was too damned cute for words.

'No,' he said again, and once more she stopped,

bright curiosity written all over her little face as she tried to work out where his voice was coming from.

She lifted her head for another song, but he told her 'no' before she'd even uttered a sound. This time she huffed, got to her feet, and slunk into her basket, her head and tail drooping.

He didn't think she'd stay there long, but it was a start, and he hastened to scour the living room for any wires she could sink her teeth into, and anything he'd be upset about if she damaged it. Obviously he couldn't move the sofa or the TV out of her reach, but he did put his Bose headphones on a high shelf, along with his phone charger and the remote control for the TV.

Deciding she'd been shut in the kitchen for long enough, he opened the door to be greeted with the same degree of enthusiasm as if he'd been gone all day, not just fifteen minutes. And she might have been in her basket but he was fairly certain she hadn't slept, so he made himself a coffee and sat on the sofa for an hour or so until it was time for her appointment, the pup sleeping peacefully, if somewhat twitchily, beside him.

Saturday morning was a busy time for the high street, and Theo recognised a few faces as he strolled down it towards the veterinary's practice. He'd lived in the town all his life, as had his parents, so it was only to be expected to see people he knew, but he hadn't anticipated the number of times he had to halt his progress for someone to pet his dog.

Puppies certainly brought out the best in people, he mused, especially one as cute as this, and even those who didn't want to stroke her smiled indulgently at the little dog. Most of them invariably glanced up and extended their smiles to him, too. He'd never been so popular!

His visit to the pet shop was no exception, as the lady behind the counter shot around it at a rate of knots when she spied Poppy. 'Ooh, she's so cute. She looks just like a teddy bear!'

With her golden curls and her button eyes, the dog certainly did. Her fur had grown a little more in the week he'd had her, and she was beginning to resemble a fluffy teddy bear.

Poppy, oblivious to how cute everyone thought she was, was more interested in the selection of doggy treats and toys on display, some of which were at her nose level. Her tail wagging enthusiastically, she nosed and sniffed, grabbing one toy before dropping it in favour of another. She reminded him of a child with pocket money to spend who had been let loose in a toy shop.

He carefully selected a couple of chews (suitable for puppies, of course!) and three new toys. His mum had bought plenty, but he wanted to buy her some himself. He also picked out some small treats suitable for using when training, and he bought more puppy pads. She was using several a day and he was almost out of them.

Poppy received a fair amount of attention in the vets' waiting room, too, and Theo felt like a proud parent when the pup was given a clean bill of health a short while later. If this was anything like having a baby, Jenson must be so excited, Theo mused. His wife was due in a couple of weeks, and while Theo couldn't imagine being a dad, having Poppy to care for was possibly the next best thing and was certainly the nearest he'd get to being a parent for a while. It was almost like a trial run at parenthood but without the eighteen years of saving up for university to consider. The pet plan he'd just signed up for was expensive enough, without the insurance he'd taken out. Kids, he knew, were a great deal more spendy.

Leaving the vet's, Theo and Poppy were sauntering back up the high street towards home, when he paused. Despite a decent breakfast, his tummy rumbled as he passed a little café which had some tables and chairs outside, and the alluring smell of freshly ground coffee and sizzling onions and garlic drew him in.

Unable to resist the temptation, he pulled out a chair at a vacant table and sat down, Poppy next to him, and looked around. No one appeared to be taking orders, although a woman did come out of the café with a tray and proceeded to clear empty cups and plates from a nearby table.

When he checked the menu, he saw that it said he was to order inside. However, there was also a sign saying no dogs allowed in the café.

At an impasse, he wondered if he should leave and find somewhere else when an idea occurred to him.

'Excuse me,' he called to a young woman sitting on the table next to him. She was alone and checking her phone, a half-empty mug of coffee in front of her.

Her expression was wary as she glanced in his direction, but immediately softened when she spotted Poppy, who was sitting on her haunches by his feet and behaving herself perfectly.

'I hate to bother you, but I'd dearly like a coffee and a crab and avocado sandwich, but they only take orders at the counter, and I can't go in because of my dog. Would you mind...?'

Her eyes lit up and she nodded, holding out her hand.

Theo gave her a twenty-pound note, and her face fell.

'Oh, I see, you want me to order and pay for you?' she said.

Theo grimaced, realising too late that she'd expected to hold Poppy while he went inside and ordered for himself. 'If that's OK?' He gave her his best hopeful expression.

'No problem,' she said, her attention on the dog. 'What's his name?'

'Poppy. She's only twelve weeks old, and she's a bit shy.'

Poppy immediately made a liar out of him by leaping to her feet the second the woman rose and proceeded to jump around her ankles.

'Oh, you are such a cute little girl. I could take you home with me, yes I could. Would you like that? You would, wouldn't you? I'd feed you chicken and dress you in cute little outfits, and you'd sleep on my bed.'

Poppy batted her with her paws and tried to lick her fingers.

The woman giggled. 'I've got to go and order some yummy food for your dad,' she told the pup. 'But I'll be back in a minute.' She straightened up.

'Can I get you another for your trouble?' Theo asked her, gesturing towards her cup.

'I'm waiting for a friend but she's late as usual, so why not? Thank you.'

'I'm the one who should be thanking you,' he protested. 'This dog-owning business is a steep learning curve. I've never had to think about whether you can take a dog into places or not, before I had her.'

'It's no bother,' she said and disappeared into the

café, returning a minute or so later with his change, and sat back down at her table.

'I take it you've not owned a dog before?' she asked.

'No, it's my first time. I am loving it though. I never would have thought I could be so besotted by a pooch.'

'I wish I had a dog, but I live by myself and my job is pretty demanding, so it wouldn't be fair on it.'

'What do you do?' He hadn't failed to notice that she'd told him she lived on her own. That didn't necessarily mean she didn't have a boyfriend though, he reminded himself, noticing how attractive she was. Long blonde hair, blue eyes, late twenties at a guess, slim, high cheekbones, upturned nose…

'I'm a grain merchant,' she replied.

'Oh.' He'd never heard of one of those before and had no idea what the job could entail.

'That's the reaction I usually get,' she grinned. 'I work for a company which buys grain from farmers and sells it on to end users, either in the UK or internationally.'

'It sounds exciting.' More exciting than trying to shoehorn quadratic equations into reluctant young minds.

'Some days it is, others not so much, like a lot of jobs. What about you?'

'I'm a teacher; maths.' He waited for the grimace. It didn't come.

'I used to enjoy maths, and it's certainly come in handy with my job.' she said.

'It often does, although I'm not sure if kids today appreciate just how essential good numeracy skills are.'

'Do you enjoy teaching?'

Hmm, how should he answer that...?

'It can be challenging,' he replied. 'Teenagers aren't often the easiest people to deal with, and as for the profession itself, there are so many changes to the curriculum, so much admin, so many non-teaching issues that we have to deal with on a daily basis, that sometimes we forget our primary purpose is to teach.' He stopped. 'I'm ranting a bit, aren't I? Sorry.'

'Don't be, it's great to be passionate about your job.'

Theo held back telling her that the passion was negative, and that he strongly disliked his chosen profession.

'My name is Marie, by the way.'

'I'm Theo, and you've already met Poppy.'

'Nice to meet you.'

The two of them smiled at each other, and Theo had no idea how long they would have continued to do so because at that moment they were interrupted by a waitress bringing their drinks and Theo's sandwich.

'Oh, there's my friend,' Marie said, waving to someone in the distance.

Disappointed, because he was quite enjoying talking

to Marie, he nodded and turned to his sandwich.

'Before she arrives, do you fancy maybe meeting for a drink sometime?' Marie asked. 'If you're free, that is? I don't want to be treading on anyone's toes.'

He put his untouched sandwich back on the plate. 'I do fancy meeting up for a drink, and yes, I am free. There's no Miss or Mrs Theo.'

'Glad to hear it. Let me have your number and I'll send you a text. You can give me a call and we'll arrange a date.'

She blushed but didn't retract the word or try to explain it away, the way he would have done. She clearly meant a date as in a *date*, not a day on a calendar, and Theo found he was very much looking forward to seeing her again.

He understood that it was down to him to make the next move, and that was fine. She'd done the brave thing by asking him out in the first place, when she didn't know the slightest thing about him.

He tried to keep himself to himself while he finished his lunch, but every so often he caught her eye and they exchanged tentative smiles. When he stood to leave, they said their goodbyes, with Marie's friend giving them bemused looks, and as he strolled back up the high street, he couldn't help thinking that his good fortune was down to Poppy. Without the dog, he never would have asked a strange woman to order his lunch.

Then another thought popped into his head.

Without Poppy, he wouldn't have met Josie, either.

CHAPTER 15

'I see you've brought the dog with you,' his mother stated the next day as Theo arrived for a plate of his mum's Sunday roast. It was beef this week, if the mouth-watering aroma was anything to go by.

'What else was I supposed to do with her?' His tone was mild, but he still hadn't totally forgiven her. He'd forgiven her for giving him Poppy, of course, but he hadn't forgiven her for assuming that she knew what was best for him. He did grudgingly admit that she might have been right about the dog bringing him out of himself – he could see that he had been stuck in a bit of a rut – but it wasn't her place to get him out of it, and he'd also never admit to her that she was right. She'd be positively insufferable if he did, and he'd never hear the end of it.

'She's grown,' Wendy said, and Theo immediately softened.

'Yes, she has,' he agreed. 'It's difficult to tell when you see her every day, but this morning I noticed she can jump onto the windowsill.'

'You let her do that?'

'No, but it doesn't stop her getting up there. She likes watching the birds.'

'I hope you're not spoiling her. There's nothing worse than a dog that doesn't know its place; isn't that right, Gerald?'

Theo and his dad exchanged knowing looks. 'That's right, love,' his father replied and pulled a face at Theo behind her back.

Theo tried not to laugh.

'What about this Jodie woman?' his mum wanted to know. 'What's going on with her?'

'It's Josie, and she's my carer. I mean, not *mine*, Poppy's. For when I'm in work.'

'You weren't in work yesterday morning,' Wendy pointed out, astutely.

'No, I was up at the crack of dawn wondering if I was doing the right thing in rehoming Poppy or not.'

'*What?* You weren't thinking of giving her away? You can't!' Wendy's mouth dropped open.

'I was, but I'm not now.'

His mother shook her head. 'I don't believe it. You take the biscuit sometimes.'

'Oh, come on, Mum, what did you expect? You

can't go giving people pets without any idea of whether they'd want one or not, and not expect repercussion.'

She huffed. 'You make it sound like I give away puppies on a regular basis.'

Theo heard his dad mutter, 'It wouldn't surprise me,' but he chose to ignore him.

'I'd never considered owning a dog, and when you showed up out of the blue with a puppy and told me it was mine, then I did what any normal person would have done – I considered my lifestyle and responsibilities, and came to the conclusion that I didn't have the time or the inclination to look after a dog.'

His mum yanked open the oven door and dragged out the roasting tin containing the joint of meat, a cloud of steam enveloping her. 'What made you change your mind?'

'Don't know,' Theo muttered and hung his head. He really, really hoped his mum wouldn't pursue the matter, because he really, really didn't want to admit that Poppy had stolen his heart and that she now had him wrapped around her paw.

'Is it because I'm right?' she demanded.

Theo's dad rolled his eyes.

'I saw that, Gerald. Here, make yourself useful and carve the beef.' She pushed the hot roasting tin across the counter. 'And you, Theo, haven't answered my question.'

'Yes, you're right,' he sighed loudly.

'Not that one – the one about Jodie.'

'*Josie*, and there's nothing going on. I paid her to keep Poppy company when I was in school last week, because you clearly weren't going to help, and she'll be walking Poppy for me in September.'

'I take it there wasn't much dog walking going on at eight o'clock on a Saturday morning.'

It was Theo's turn to roll his eyes. 'Whatever.'

Wendy brandished a spoon at him. 'Don't you 'whatever' me, my boy – you're not too old for a good telling off.'

'What are you going to do? Ground me? Stop my pocket money?' Theo sniggered and his dad joined in.

Wendy shot Gerald a warning look and his dad put on a serious expression, but as soon as his mum turned her attention back to the hob, Gerald sniggered again, albeit silently.

'I don't care what you say, I reckon there's more going on than you're telling us. What do you think?' Wendy aimed the question at her husband, who shrugged.

'There's not, and I'll tell you why,' Theo said. 'I've got a date with someone else.'

His mum's eyes narrowed and she pursed her lips. 'Who?'

'Her name is Marie and she's a grain merchant.' He hoped his mum wouldn't ask for further details, because he simply didn't have any. So to stop her in her tracks, he added, 'Don't ask me anything else. I'll tell you more about her when I'm ready.'

'How long have you been seeing her?'

Theo shook his head and mimed zipping his lips together.

'Where—?'

'Nope. Not another word.'

His mother snorted in disgust, but thankfully she allowed him to change the subject to Poppy's first puppy training session on Tuesday evening. But as he was telling his parents about it, he was also frantically planning on what to say when he called Marie.

The fact that he wished it was Josie he was about to ask out on a date, hadn't passed him by, either.

CHAPTER 16

'Is it OK if I come with you?' Josie asked, when he told her about the puppy training class.

'Er, yes, I suppose. But it *is* for puppies,' he pointed out. He wasn't sure of Crumble's age, but the spaniel was definitely more than a year old.

'I know, I just like being around puppies, and I can hardly bring Crumble along. It would be even worse if I turned up without a dog at all,' she joked.

So that was the reason the pair of them plus Poppy were sitting in a half circle in the community centre hall, armed with poo bags, wet wipes and kitchen roll and praying that it wouldn't be their dog who had the inevitable accident. That was what Theo was thinking anyway; he had no idea what was going through Josie's mind, but from her indulgent expression, she was in her element.

'Are there any jobs working specifically with

puppies?' Theo asked her, when she exclaimed over yet another young mutt.

'I'm not sure – fostering guide dogs, maybe? But how could you possibly let them go to start the next part of their training? I know I couldn't; I'd get too attached.'

No surprise – he could see she was attached to Poppy, so goodness knows what she'd be like if she was fostering a pup 24/7.

To be fair to her, she didn't make any attempt to take a turn at the actual training bit, appearing content to sit on the sidelines and watch as he tried to persuade Poppy that coming to him when she was called and receiving a treat as a reward was better than dashing off to say hello to everyone.

He listened to the instructor as she informed the group that it was imperative that the pups learned the recall command, as one day their lives may depend on it. Which was why Theo was determined Poppy would come back to him at his first ask, and not after calling her numerous times.

It was going to take some work, he realised, as the lure of a beagle pup proved too much for her, and she scooted off.

The whole lesson could be called organised mayhem, as puppies and owners darted here, there and everywhere, all of them having huge amounts of fun.

Every now and again, he heard Josie's unmistakable laugh as she giggled at a dog's antics, and he was glad he'd brought her along. She was having a whale of a time and thoroughly enjoying herself – as they all were. If someone had told him a few weeks ago that he'd shortly spend a Tuesday evening running around a community centre after a small furry pup and loving every second of it, he'd have thought they were mad.

He'd had his eye on what looked suspiciously like another Cockapoo for a while now, when its owner came within speaking distance. 'Cockapoo?' he asked the woman breathlessly as he caught Poppy and put her back on the lead.

'Yeah, yours too? Aren't they lovely? So good-natured, but my God are they lively.'

Theo, having limited experience of any other dogs, smiled and nodded in vague agreement. The woman he was talking to gathered her creamy coloured dog up and cuddled it.

'How old?' she asked.

'Twelve weeks, Yours?'

'Sixteen weeks. My old dog passed away a few months ago, and I swore I wouldn't have another, but the house was too empty without a pooch in it. I didn't think I'd love this little guy as much as I do, but he's stolen my heart and I can't imagine being without him now.'

'Me too! I've only had Poppy eleven days, but it seems like she's always been in my life.'

Theo and the woman smiled their understanding at each other, and he thought how lovely her eyes were – a clear hazel, large and rimmed with thick lashes. She had a generous mouth and a ready smile, and was rather attractive.

Instinctively he glanced at her left hand which was curled around the pup. No ring.

'What made you decide on a Cockapoo?' she asked.

He screwed his face up. 'My mother. She bought her for me.'

'Oh, what a lovely present. Birthday?'

'Not exactly. What about you?'

'My daughter, Chloe – she's six – saw a picture of one on the telly and set her heart on it. My last dog was a Jack Russell, and I think it was the fact that when they're little Cockapoos look like teddy bears which attracted her to them. And I like them because they don't shed as much as most other dogs. With Clive I was forever picking hairs off my clothes.'

'I take it Clive was your Jack Russell, not your other half?' Subtle, Theo – not.

'I don't have a other half,' she replied. 'It's just me and Chloe, and now Teddy.'

'I bet your daughter named him,' Theo said, with a laugh.

'Yeah, she did.' The woman shook her head fondly. 'I'll bring her with me next week; she was gutted to miss this first session but her father has taken her to Cornwall for a few days.'

Her tone when she said "father" told him that there was no love lost between her and her child's dad.

'I think someone wants you,' the woman said looking over Theo's shoulder.

He turned to see Josie waving at him.

He waved back. 'That's my friend, Josie. She walks Poppy for me when I'm in work,' he explained, not sure why he felt he needed to clarify his relationship with her to this stranger, but he did so anyway. It wasn't as though he intended to get to know her any better – he was a one woman at a time kinda guy, and that woman was Marie, who'd agreed to a date on Thursday.

Thursdays, according to Jenson's theory on dating (he seemed to think he was an expert, even though he was the one who had been coupled up the longest out of the *Don't Tell the Missus* gang), was the best day of the week for a first date. Not as significant as a Friday or a Saturday, not as pathetic as a Sunday or Monday. According to him, no one dated on Sundays or Mondays, and Tuesdays and Wednesdays were reserved for those dates where you thought you might need a get-out-clause of having to get up early for work, if you wanted to end the date early. When Theo had pointed out that the same could be said for Thursday, Jenson had argued that it could go both ways. If the date was a wash-out, then you could plead an early end to it because of the work situation; but if it was going well, then you could argue that you only had to get out of bed early one more time that week before a lie-in on the weekend. According to him, it was a win-win situation.

Theo wasn't exactly sure why he'd suggested Thursday (he was a teacher and it was the school hols, for goodness sake, so Jenson's daft theory didn't apply), but it seemed a good choice of day. It was a casual drink, that was all. Nothing too heavy.

'She's still waving,' Teddy's mum pointed out.

Eh? Theo looked again.

Josie was definitely waving, and when she saw she'd got his attention, she pointed at him.

'Me?' he mouthed, pointing at himself.

'Poppy,' she mouthed back, pointing again, and when he glanced down at his dog, he saw why.

She'd done a big poo while he'd been busy talking to the other owner, and was standing next to the noxious pile looking remarkably pleased with herself.

With a sigh, Theo trudged back to where Josie was sitting and handed her the lead, while he went to clear up the pup's mess.

Oh, the joys of owning a dog, he thought sarcastically. But the woman was right – he simply couldn't imagine being without Poppy now; the house would be too empty without her. His life and his heart would be too empty without her.

CHAPTER 17

His date with Marie wasn't going well. On the other hand, it wasn't going badly, either. Theo couldn't put his finger on what was wrong with it, though. Marie was pretty, friendly, easy to talk to, funny, intelligent... In fact, everything he could have wanted if he'd made a list of essential attributes needed for his ideal woman.

But there was something missing... a spark, a connection? He wasn't sure what. All he knew was he wasn't feeling it – whatever *it* was.

It felt like he was out for a drink with a friend or a work colleague. The pair of them had little in common at first glance, but normally that wouldn't bother him. Couples often didn't have a great deal in common (take Jenson and his missus, for instance) but that could come with time, as they knew more about each other, and as they forged memories and experienced things together.

But that was the problem – he didn't think he wanted to experience anything else with Marie. He didn't particularly want to get to know her, and he certainly didn't want to forge any lasting memories with her.

He was prepared to admit that the problem was his. He couldn't seem to stop mentioning Poppy and after the first couple of times, he noticed Marie's expression glazing over. She did perk up a bit when he recounted the poop in the middle of the community centre episode, but rather than finding it amusing, she looked mildly nauseated.

For all her fussing and baby talk when she'd met Poppy last weekend, she wasn't a doggy person. If the thought of cleaning up poo made her go green about the gills, then she wasn't the woman for him.

Theo suspected she wouldn't be the woman for him regardless, no matter how much she failed to flinch at the less enjoyable aspects of dog ownership.

Both of them were equally relieved to call it a night after only a couple of drinks and, after a desultory and rather awkward goodbye peck on the cheek, Theo headed home, anxious to see how Poppy had got on without him. Although, for one thing she hadn't been on her own – his parents had dog-sat – and for another, the camera in the kitchen was still on, and he'd taken the odd sneaky peek at it while he was supposed to be paying attention to Marie.

He wasn't proud of the way he'd acted, but he hadn't been able to help himself. Besides, he'd caught his mum rooting about in his cupboards, taking everything out, giving the shelves a wipe over, and putting everything back in a totally different place – which meant he'd never be able to find anything ever again. But the really telling thing was that, unless he'd witnessed her doing it, he probably wouldn't have noticed that his shelves had been scrubbed to within an inch of their lives, until he went to look for something and it wasn't where he expected it to be.

'How did it go?' his mum asked, after he'd spent a few minutes saying hello to Poppy, who was ecstatic to see him.

'OK, I suppose. We didn't have a great deal in common. I don't think I'm her type.'

'She must have seen something in you to go out with you in the first place. What did you do to put her off? You didn't talk about work or football all evening, did you?'

'No, I did not. I talked about Poppy, and a bit about my job, and… oh, I told her about Poppy disgracing herself at the puppy training class and—'

'When I said you needed livening up a bit, I didn't mean for you to swap talking about work for wittering on about the dog.'

'I don't witter. Old ladies witter.'

'Have you heard yourself?'

'Mum!' To his own ears, he sounded suspiciously like the way he had sounded when he was a kid and she'd done something to embarrass him. 'Anyway, it was because of Poppy that I had a date with her in the first place,' he added.

'Oh, so you're treating that poor defenceless little puppy as a babe magnet, are you?'

'Babe magnet?' Theo chortled. 'Honestly, Mum? Have you been talking to Jenson?'

His mum scowled, but his dad, bless him, just looked resigned. He was used to her after God knows how many years of marriage, and Theo knew that he preferred not to get involved most of the time.

Both Jenson and his mum were right though; Poppy did hold a certain attraction for the opposite sex, no matter what their age, and he'd already been given a phone number by one woman, had gone on a date with another, and had possibly got some interest from Robyn, the supply teacher in work. Which reminded him – he still had her phone number. He could always give her a call; at least they'd have their jobs in common if nothing else. It was too late to contact her this evening however, so he promised himself he'd ring her tomorrow.

After his parents left, giving lots of kisses to the dog

on their way out and a quick hug for him (great, he'd been relegated to second position behind the dog in their affections), he grabbed his phone and checked the *Don't Tell the Missus* WhatsApp group.

The most recent notification was from Jenson complaining about being woken up five times a night by the need of his heavily pregnant wife to visit the bathroom, or wanting a drink, or being unable to sleep because she was uncomfortable, or the baby was kicking, or… The list went on, supplemented by his childless mates ribbing him and the commiserations and gleeful warnings of "it'll only get worse" from those in the group who'd already been blessed with the patter of tiny feet.

For a wild moment Theo wondered if he should chip in with tales of sleepless nights due to a puppy howling, before common sense got the better of him. His doggy problems were hardly in the same league.

Jenson: *I need gin.*

Dave: *You don't like gin.*

Jenson: *Not for me, for Bella.*

Archie: *Is it allowed?*

Jenson: *If it isn't, it should be! I'll be glad when the baby is out.*

Henry: *It won't get any better. It'll get worse.*

Jenson: *Cheers, mate, that's really cheered me up. Anyone got anything constructive to say?*

Henry: **Weetabix is a close relative of cement.**

Archie: **???**

Henry: **Dries solid. You need a sandblaster to get the stuff off.**

Archie: **?????? WTF?**

Henry: **Just trying to give advice. He asked.**

Morgan: **I don't think he meant that sort of advice.**

Morgan had been absent from the group for a while, so it was nice to have him back.

Theo: **Hi, Morgan.** Followed by a waving hand emoji.

Jenson: **Henry, you're not helping. I should have tried to talk her into having a cat instead.**

Theo: **I've got a dog.**

Dave: **I thought you said it belonged to your parents? Or have you moved back in with your mum? Mummy's boy.**

Theo: **Get lost! I'm not living with my mother, and the dog is mine.**

Dave: **The cock and poo one?**

The group chat was bombarded with laughing face emojis and other assorted insults; they obviously hadn't forgotten his earlier misunderstanding and he guessed he'd probably get ribbed about it for some time to come. Possibly for the rest of his life.

Jenson: **Stick to dogs, mate. Easier.'**

Theo wasn't so sure about that but then what did he know about it, being single and childless? And if this last date of his was anything to go by, it looked like he was going to stay that way for a while yet.

CHAPTER 18

Theo was getting used to early mornings since Poppy had come into his life. Before Poppy, he'd not risen before seven-thirty on a school day, and on the days he was off, he wouldn't surface before ten a.m. normally, sometimes later.

Having a small pup had changed all that. Neither her little bladder nor her tummy could last beyond roughly five-thirty, so up he'd get and the day would begin with a quick visit outside followed by breakfast – for the dog, that is. He'd have his own breakfast later, when his stomach had woken up.

He was starting to enjoy the peace and quiet of an early morning stroll. The world was new and fresh, reborn almost. Today was no exception and the sky was a clear bright blue, the sun already well risen and there wasn't a cloud to be seen. Birdsong filled the air, and the trees and bushes were alive with twittering and fluttering.

The park was generally empty at this time in the morning (not even the most die-hard of dog walkers seemed to be out before six-thirty) and he felt as though it was his own private garden. Except for the ever-present birds and the occasional bold squirrel (it knew that Poppy was never going to catch it), the pair of them had the place to themselves. It was possibly even too early for most insects, although the buzz of an intrepid bee could be heard amongst the flower beds.

Josie would be taking Poppy out for a walk around midday, because he wanted the pup to be in the same routine now as she would be in come September. He intended to walk her first thing – which was lovely when it was a day like today in the middle of summer, but he didn't know how he'd feel about taking her out on a wet, cold, dark December morning – Josie would walk her around lunchtime, and he' take her out again when he arrived home. That was the plan anyway, and he hoped it would work.

'Hello, you're early,' he said, spotting Crumble as he dashed through a flower bed to greet them. Poppy bounced around with joy at seeing her friend and the two dogs were soon grass-deep in a game of chase.

Crumble's owner walked around some large bushes and came into view, and Theo was struck anew by how lovely she was.

If he was honest, Marie was the more striking of the two women, but something about Josie had a hold of him and refused to let go. A bit like Poppy with her toys when they were playing tug. She had strong jaws for such a little thing, he thought, smiling.

'You look happy,' Josie observed coming closer. 'I thought you didn't do mornings.'

'I didn't used to, but with Poppy I don't have any choice, and I'm starting to appreciate being up and about when the rest of the world is asleep. How about you? I haven't seen you in the park at this time of day before.'

'I'm not usually, but Crumble heard a noise outside at about four this morning and started barking. By the time I'd got up to see what it was, I was wide awake and couldn't get back to sleep. So here I am.'

Theo might love having the park to himself, but he was delighted to see Josie too, and he thoroughly enjoyed walking part of the way with her. She was easy to be with, and she didn't seem to be one of those people who felt the need to fill any and all silences with inane chatter. She appeared just as content to stroll quietly, as she was to speak.

He found his thoughts kept turning to her throughout the morning after he'd arrived home and as much as he tried to shoo her from his mind, she kept popping back into it. It didn't help that he was at a loss for something to do. While Poppy had a nap, he'd done what needed to be done around the house, then when she'd woken up he'd played tug with her, followed by fetch (which involved him throwing the ball and Poppy refusing to bring it back), then chase, until she finally settled down, tired out again, to chomp on a chew.

He was exhausted himself and felt as though it should be late afternoon rather than just coming up to lunchtime, so he was glad when Josie arrived to take Poppy for her midday jaunt. It meant he could eat lunch in peace while watching an episode of something on the TV. It seemed to have been a long time since he'd watched anything without being interrupted by a furry little hooligan wanting to play, and he couldn't remember which series he'd been immersed in. The last thing he could remember watching was John Wick, but that was a film not a series, and he'd not made it to the end on that occasion because that was the evening he'd become the proud owner of a small dog.

He was just drifting off to sleep in the armchair when Josie returned, rousing him from what might have been a quite substantial nap.

'Oh, my God, what's happened?' he asked when he opened the door. He'd never seen Josie looking so upset. Actually, he'd never see Josie looking upset at all. Right now, her lips were drawn into a tight line, her chin was wobbling and her eyes were brimming with tears. He stepped to the side to let her enter and ushered her into the living room.

'Mrs Barnett who lives a few doors away from me has had her poor little Sugarplum stolen.'

'Pardon?'

'Sugarplum is a very sweet, very loving and quite expensive Pomeranian,' Josie explained, her voice hitching.

'That's a dog, isn't it?' He'd been imagining some kind of fruit tree. 'How did it happen?'

'Apparently it happened last night, or rather, in the early hours of this morning. Remember me telling you that Crumble was barking at something outside? That was probably when they were stealing Sugarplum.'

'Is Mrs Barnett all right? Do the police know who did it? Did they break in? Was anything else taken?'

Josie hitched in a deep breath, blinking as Theo fired questions at her. 'Mrs Barnett's fine, and no, there was no break-in. She had to get up to go to the loo – Mrs Barnett, that is, not Sugarplum – but she let the Pom out at the same time because she'll sleep on a bit in the morning if she's had a wee.'

'Mrs Barnett will?'

'No, the dog. Anyway, she pottered about in the kitchen for a bit, making herself a cup of tea to take back to bed, when she realised that Sugarplum hadn't come back in.' Josie paused and wiped a tear from her cheek. 'I'm sorry to get so upset, but she's quite elderly and rather deaf, and she's got terribly bad arthritis.'

'The dog?' Theo hazarded a guess, wondering how cruel you'd have to be to separate an elderly, ailing dog from its owner.

'Mrs Barnett. That's why she didn't hear anyone climb over her gate and steal Sugarplum.'

'Surely it must be kids,' Theo said, knowing it most probably wasn't. Any kid worth his or her salt, would be tucked up in bed at that time in the morning and doing the teenagery thing of staying there until midday.

'She was targeted.'

'Mrs Barnett?'

'The dog. They knew exactly what they were after and the best time to pounce. Mrs Barnett is a creature of habit, and she nearly always wakes about that time and lets Sugarplum out to have a wee. They must have been watching the house.' Josie shivered and rubbed her arms. 'I just wish I'd gone to investigate, but all I did was look out of the window and when I couldn't see anything, I assumed Crumble must have heard a cat or a fox, and I went back upstairs. Thank God I didn't let Crumble out at the same time, or they might have stolen him, too. And I honestly couldn't bear that.'

She gulped and a few more tears trickled down her face.

Theo felt as though his heart had turned to ice. Just the thought of someone stealing Poppy made him go cold all over.

He stepped towards Josie and wrapped her in a hug. He wasn't normally a touchy-feely person and could no way be described as a hugger, but he felt they could both do with one.

'God, I hope the police find whoever did this,' she continued her voice muffled against his chest. 'The officers who she reported it to said there had been a spate of dog-knapping recently and they didn't hold out a great deal of hope. Apparently, the thieves are stealing to order, and they know the breeds that cost the most, and Pomeranians are rather expensive besides being cute.'

Josie slowly moved out of the circle of his arms and gave him a wobbly smile. 'Speaking of cute, your Poppy gets a great deal of attention, doesn't she? I think my favourite comment so far is that she's like a real-live teddy bear. Seriously, though, there are some unscrupulous people about and if they can steal an old lady's sole companion, they wouldn't think twice about nabbing Poppy.'

'Thanks for the warning. I never let her out in the garden on her own, and I hope the six-foot wall and wooden gate would keep any thieves out. I dread to think what I'd do if anyone took her.' Images of John

Wick going on the rampage after a thug killed his dog and stole his car, careened through his mind. He could fully understand where the guy was coming from, even if it was only a film and the whole thing was over-the-top and outrageous. Theo didn't condone violence in any shape or form, but he'd be seriously angry if anyone endangered his dog.

He'd get a better bolt for the garden gate, he vowed, and maybe an outside light, the kind that was motion sensitive. It would be a good idea to have one anyway for the winter when it was dark at four p.m. And he was also thankful that he hadn't acted on his dog flap idea. After hearing Josie's news, he didn't want to let Poppy go outside unsupervised, even if it was into a secure garden.

He saw Josie and Crumble out, asking if there was anything he could do to help Mrs Barnett (flyers? internet searches? knocking on doors? anything...), and his heart was heavy. The poor old lady; she must be distraught. He couldn't even begin to imagine what she must be going through, and instinctively he picked Poppy up and gave her a huge cuddle, burying his face in the fluff on the top of her head.

As he hugged his pup, he remembered the feel of Josie in his arms. He hadn't thought about it at the time because he'd been too busy concentrating on her news and the fact that she was understandably upset. It had upset him, too. But now that the hug was over and the woman in question wasn't standing in front of him filling his senses, he realised how much he'd enjoyed it. It had felt right. More than right – it had been perfect. She'd fitted into his embrace as though she'd been made for him.

For a second, he wished he was going on a date with Josie instead of Robyn, but common sense kicked in before his wayward thoughts did any more damage to his equilibrium. Josie was off limits for the very same reason he'd waited until term ended before he'd called Robyn. Mixing business with pleasure was never a good idea, and he would hate for things to go south with Josie because he'd made a pass at her and she wasn't interested. It would make her being employed by him to walk his dog incredibly awkward, and Poppy was used to her now – he genuinely didn't want to have to look for another dog carer.

It was best to leave things just the way they were – a business relationship. They could be friends within the parameters of that relationship, but nothing more.

He knew in his head that it was the right decision; all he had to do now was to convince his heart, because he had an awful feeling that Josie Wilde had crept inside and had taken up residence there.

CHAPTER 19

Oh, no… Theo debated whether to turn back, cross over to the other side of the road, or stride past and pretend he hadn't seen the five Year 10 lads who were arsing about at the bus stop.

In the end, he did none of those things. He was the adult here, he was their teacher – he shouldn't have to avoid them, even though he would have loved to do exactly that. These five were the worst in the class; if there was any trouble, any low-level (or higher-level) disruption, one or more of them would be at the heart of it. Although to be fair to Ronnie Elder, Theo didn't think he'd set eyes on the kid since the second week in October. The boy was an infrequent attender, despite numerous interventions and support packages put in place for the family. Neither the kid's mum, nor the child himself, could see the point in going to school. Ronnie didn't like it, and he was a nightmare when he was there, forever in detention or being excluded. The school, the local education department, Ronnie and his mum had reached an impasse, and Theo couldn't see anything changing in September.

'Awright, sir?' Ronnie called as Theo and Poppy drew closer.

Heck, that was an improvement – the lad had called him "sir". Theo was surprised Ronnie recognised him, it had been so long since he'd clapped eyes on any of his teachers.

'Grand, thanks, Ronnie. And you? How's your mum?' Ms Elder was a single parent who was trying to do her best as she saw it. Theo had to admire her for that, even if they didn't agree on what "the best" was.

'She's OK.' His glance cut to the side, as though he was daring any of the other boys to contradict him, and Theo guessed that something was up.

'That's good,' he said, neutrally. No doubt he'd get to hear about it on the grapevine. Maybe not straight away, but certainly when term started – kids talked, their parents talked, and in a small town like Pershore, things soon got around. All he hoped was that it was nothing more serious than Ms Elder having a new boyfriend who Ronnie didn't like, which was usually the case.

'Will I see you in my class in September?' he asked the teenager.

'Depends, don't it?'

'On what?'

'Stuff.'

That was as clear as mud, but Theo wasn't about to ask what the "stuff" was. He probably wouldn't get a reply, and if he did, he mightn't want to hear it. There was only so much teachers and the school could do to help their pupils, and Theo often felt out of his depth when it came to the issues some of the kids faced. Pershore wasn't a deprived area by any stretch of the imagination, but like most other places it had its fair share of problems, and these were reflected in the home lives of some of the pupils he taught.

'That your dog?' one of the other boys asked. Tim Hogan was perched on top of the bus shelter roof, sitting there with his legs crossed and a cigarette in his hand.

'Yes, her name is Poppy and she's a Cockapoo.' He was prepared for the sniggers, but remarkably they didn't materialise.

'Sound. My sister's got a Sproodle and it's as mad a box of frogs.'

'Sproodle?' Theo raised his eyebrows.

'Springer spaniel and poodle. Its effing nuts, I mean, totally tonto. Is yours daft?'

'Not really, she's still a baby so she can be a bit lively.'

'Let us have a stroke.' Tim stubbed out his cigarette and climbed down.

Theo stared at him.

'Please, sir,' the boy added reluctantly, remembering his manners.

'Go ahead, but be gentle, she's only three months old,' Theo said, not wanting any of the kids to touch his dog, but also realising he was being silly. The boys might be horrors in school, but they were only teenagers and none of them would deliberately harm her. He recognised that he was feeling over-protective and over-cautious after hearing the news of Mrs Barnett's Sugarplum

Tim held out his hand and Poppy delicately sniffed the boy's fingers before deciding he was OK and swiping at him with her pink tongue.

'She's nice, ain't she?'

'I think so.'

'Can I have a go?'

Theo raised his eyebrows again, this time in surprise. It was Ronnie who had spoken. The lad would have been the last person Theo would have expected to want to pet a puppy.

'Please?' Ronnie added, and Theo smiled noting that the "sir" was missing. He didn't care – he'd managed to get Ronnie Elder to say "please".

'Go ahead, but the same thing applies.'

One by one the boys took turns to gently pet Poppy, who was in her element at all the attention and was being exceptionally cute.

For once Theo didn't hear the "cute" word – he didn't think teenage boys knew such a word existed – but the pup did receive lots of compliments and more than one comment about her looking like a teddy bear. It was the most animated he'd seen these kids ever. It just shows you what they can be like when something interests them, he thought; it was a pity maths didn't elicit the same response.

'She's a bit of a girl's dog, Mr Martin,' Cory Denham said, peeping slyly up at him from beneath an artfully floppy fringe. The rest of his hair was close-cropped, with a pattern shaved into it. It was quite a work of art.

'Do you think?' Theo's response was mild; there was no way he was going to rise to the bait.

'Yeah, I think. I prefer, like, Pit Bulls and, like, Staffies.'

'They shed a lot though,' Theo pointed out.

'You what?'

'Lose their hair, usually all over your clothes.' Theo didn't know enough about those breeds to know whether they did or didn't, but he hazarded a guess.

'So?'

'I can't be bothered to pick hairs off my clothes every day. Poppy hardly loses any hair.'

'He's right, Cozza,' Tim said. 'My sister's dog don't moult. It's why she got him.'

'Still girly,' Cory muttered, but with far less conviction and the belligerence had disappeared.

'I think Mr Martin's dog is lit,' Ronnie said, and the other boys nodded.

Theo had no idea what Ronnie had just said, but he guessed it must be a good thing. Poppy, and therefore he himself, seemed to have Ronnie's approval – which was a miracle in itself.

Not wanting to push his luck and wanting to leave while the going was good, Theo said his goodbyes and ambled away. He felt as though a brisk walk was in order, but kids like those could smell weakness and he didn't want to give any of them the slightest opportunity to play up in class.

As he strolled away, imagining five pairs of eyes boring into his back (not that he had any intention of turning around to check), he heard Ronnie say, 'Mr Martin's all right for a prof.'

For a second, he wondered what Ronnie meant, then it occurred to him – prof... professor... teacher – and he smiled. That was possibly the most positive encounter he'd ever had with any of those lads, Ronnie in particular.

And it had all been down to Poppy.

CHAPTER 20

Discussing school life was all well and good, but having little else to talk about on a date was rather disconcerting and extremely disappointing. Theo did have fun though, swapping horror stories with Robyn. Although she was still in her first year of teaching, the fact that she was on supply meant that she'd already built up a wealth of experience at other schools, the reputation of some of those where she'd worked being well known as having behavioural issues. Robert Crouch lay somewhere in the middle – it wasn't the best and neither was it the worst. It did worry him though, that she'd been reduced to tears by a relatively well-behaved Year 7 class.

'Have you any plans for the rest of the summer?' he asked, after the school stories had been exhausted.

'Not really. Try to recharge my batteries ready for the next academic year. You?'

'House-train my dog, but that's about it. I've got no plans to go anywhere.'

'Oh, that's right, you've got a puppy, haven't you?'

'Yeah, she's grown a bit since the last time you saw her. Want to see?'

'Go on then, I love all those cute photos of puppies on Facebook.'

It wasn't a photo Theo showed her – it was live footage from the camera in his kitchen. He'd not asked his parents to dog-sit on this occasion. Instead, he'd done his best to wear the pup out before he set off for his date, having taken her on her longest walk yet (not too far though, because she only had little legs and was still very young), followed by a prolonged play session. His tactics seemed to have worked, because she was curled up in a ball in her basket with her nose buried in her tail.

Robyn squinted at his phone.

'Aw, that's a pity,' he said. 'it looks like she's asleep.' Satisfied that the dog was behaving herself, he found some decent photos and showed those to Robyn instead. While she made suitable appreciative noises, Theo was relieved that he'd got away with checking on Poppy without appearing to be rude or without having to resort to nipping off to the loo.

The conversation continued to stagger along, not awkwardly exactly but certainly not flowing in the way he'd hoped. Unless he was very much mistaken (and he could so easily be) he got the impression that Robyn really liked him. She kept lowering her lashes and peeping out at him from underneath them, or reaching across the table to touch his arm. Once or twice she'd leaned forward and placed a hand on his knee.

Unfortunately, it hadn't elicited any response from him in the trouser department. All he'd felt was slightly uncomfortable and a tad embarrassed, which certainly didn't bode well for any future relationship.

What was wrong with him? Robyn was pretty, intelligent, effervescent… yet he'd reacted to her as though she was one of his mate's partners, in whom he had zero romantic interest. She'd make a great friend, though.

In desperation, at the end of the evening, he kissed her.

They were strolling towards her house because, like the gentleman he was, Theo had offered to walk her home, and she'd slipped her arm through his and cuddled into him. The gesture wasn't as intimate as holding hands, but he felt she was making it clear that any further moves on his part wouldn't be rejected.

It wasn't fully dark yet (Theo didn't want to stay out too long because of Poppy) but the sun had set and the sky above the distant Malvern Hills was a glorious display of orange and pink. They'd agreed on a pub in the village of Kempsey where Robyn lived, so only one of them would have to drive, and the walk from the pub where he'd parked his car to her house, was a pleasant one. A few stars were shining to the east and the air was warm and perfumed from the jasmine spilling over a garden fence as they sauntered past. Theo trailed his free hand across the blooms, releasing yet more intoxicating scent into the night.

It should have been romantic...

And that was when he kissed Robyn.

With the heady perfume all around them, he halted and turned slowly to face her, slipping his arm out of hers and sliding it around her waist, drawing her to him. She stepped forwards and wrapped her arms around his neck, tilting her head to look up at him. The invitation was clear, and her mouth parted a little and she closed her eyes.

Theo lowered his head, his lips when they met hers were light and tentative, and his own lids drifted shut. She was warm and soft, and tasted vaguely of the gin she'd drunk. It was quite pleasant.

Without warning, Josie's face popped into his mind and his eyes flew open.

No, that wasn't good... To be kissing one woman while thinking about another, simply wouldn't do at all. And what was with the "pleasant" thing? Surely a kiss should be more than *pleasant*?

Annoyed with himself, he groaned.

Robyn's arm's tightened around him, and as she pressed herself against him it was enough to make him flinch.

It was no good; this had to stop. It wasn't right to keep up the pretence. He didn't feel anything for Robyn and leading her on was unforgiveable.

Pulling his lips from hers he let go of her, then realising he'd been a bit too abrupt as a hurt expression clouded her face, he said, 'I'm sorry… I… it's just…'

Just *what*, he asked himself.

But he knew the answer to his own question – *Josie*.

CHAPTER 21

'Come in and have a look at my new kitchen,' Josie offered, when he dropped Poppy off for one of her twice-weekly visits to her carer's house.

Theo hesitated. It wasn't that he didn't want to spend more time with Josie, and he would quite like to see her kitchen because she appeared to be so proud of it; it was more that he didn't trust himself around her.

He wasn't going to jump her bones or make a total tit of himself by asking her out – he simply didn't want to open his heart up to her any more than it was already. In the same way Poppy had done, Josie had winkled her way into his life and his emotions so gradually that he hadn't noticed it was happening until it was too late.

Poppy he could deal with.

He wasn't so sure about Josie. He'd repeatedly gone

over all the reasons why asking her out would be a bad idea, and those reasons were still valid. But as long as he kept his feelings to himself, Josie need never be aware of them and their relationship could continue in the same vein as now. It would get easier when he was back in work he told himself, because she'd be calling in to pick up Poppy when he wasn't at home. And except for bumping into each other now and again in the park, they wouldn't be having a great deal of contact. All he had to do was get through the next three or so weeks until term started back up, and he could relax.

'You don't have to,' Josie said, sounding deflated, and Theo realised he'd been standing on her doorstep dithering for much longer than was polite.

Flustered, he said, 'Sorry, I was miles away. Of course I'd like to see your kitchen.' And he would, because it meant spending more time with Josie.

Bugger – he was doing it again; deciding to keep her at arms' length one minute, then doing the exact opposite the next, whether it was having her image leap into his mind while he was supposed to be on a date with someone else, or electing to spend longer in her company when he knew it wasn't going to do his turbulent feelings any good.

'What do you think?' she asked, after leading him down the hallway and into the room at the back of the house.

He hadn't seen it before so he didn't have anything to compare it to, but it did look lovely (just like her).

Stop it…

White and clean with crisp lines and lots of worktop space and cupboards, it positively gleamed, and was far neater than his kitchen had ever been. He wondered if the rest of her house was as neat; the upstairs for instance…?

'I haven't cooked in it yet,' she admitted. 'Unless shoving bread in the toaster counts as cooking. You put me to shame.'

'Do I? I expect you're a great cook.'

'Nah, not half as good as you.'

He knew those darned enchiladas would come back to haunt him. 'I bet you're better than me.'

'I can prove that I'm not, if you like. How about coming to mine for dinner tomorrow night?'

Oh, no, that wouldn't be a good idea at all. Being in her house for something as intimate as a meal, wouldn't feel right. Or rather, it would feel far *too* right for his liking. He couldn't explain it, but the thought of it gave him goose bumps. He'd feel more in control if she came to his.

'How about I cook for you again?' The words were out of his mouth before they'd been processed by his brain.

'You don't want to risk my cooking, do you?' she teased. 'And I don't blame you. You're on, if you let me bring the wine and the dessert.'

'Great!' He sounded far more enthusiastic than he felt, and it wasn't only because he'd be putting himself out there again. It was also because he had no idea what to cook or how to cook it, and tearing a plastic lid off a ready-meal wasn't an option.

Which was why he hot-footed it to his mum's house as soon as he said goodbye to Josie.

'Where's Poppy?' his mother demanded when he barged into the house.

'I thought you'd be in work.'

He'd *hoped* she'd be in work, because he'd been planning on raiding her well-stocked freezer, knowing that she often cooked meals in batches, like sauces for spaghetti for instance, her own lasagne, and casseroles, to name a few. His mum was famed for being organised.

She narrowed her eyes at him. 'Which begs the question, why are you here if you thought I wasn't going to be?'

'Um…'

'And you still haven't answered my question – where's Poppy?'

'Look, I might have thought about finding another home for her in the beginning, but not anymore, so stop being so suspicious. I can leave her in the house on her own, you know; she's not a child.'

His mum continued to study him. He knew that she knew he was fibbing.

He caved. 'She's at Josie's.'

'Oh, yeah…?'

'I've explained it to you before; I want Poppy to get used to being with Josie for when I'm back at work. Which reminds me – what are you doing here?'

'I live here.'

He sighed. His mum could be hard work sometimes. 'You know what I mean.'

'I've reduced my hours.'

'You have? You could have mentioned this before I shelled out a small fortune on a dog sitter.'

His mum gave him an inscrutable smile. 'You haven't said why *you're* here,' she reminded him.

'Oh, it's ah… nothing. No reason.'

Wendy folded her arms and glared at him. 'I can tell when you're up to something, Theo Aloysius Martin, so don't try to pull the wool over my eyes.'

Theo winced; he hated when she used his full name. *Aloysius* – what the hell had his parents been thinking!

He drew himself up to his full height and tried for a dignified expression. 'I'm having someone to dinner tomorrow evening, and I was hoping you'd be able to suggest a main course.'

'Difficult to suggest anything if I'm not here,' his mother pointed out. 'You were hoping to pinch something from my freezer, weren't you?'

Brazening it out, Theo replied, 'Guilty. Now, do you have anything?'

'Lamb shank, and you can cook it yourself from scratch.' She drew out a package from the fridge and gave it to him. 'You'll need red wine, beef stock, tomato puree, garlic, onions— What?'

'I might have the wine, as for the rest…'

'Buy it. Now, you sear the lamb— *What*?'

'Sear?'

'Never mind. Give me the meat.'

Theo handed it over. Maybe he'd cook a steak. You couldn't go wrong with steak, and he'd buy a ready prepared salad to go with it.

His mum got her heavy frying pan out of the cupboard and plonked it down on the hob with a clatter. 'Who did you say was coming for dinner?'

'I didn't.'

'Who is it?'

She wouldn't let up until he told her, and there was no point in saying it was Jenson because for one thing, inviting his mate for dinner would be too weird for words, and for another if he and Jenson were to have a meal together at his place it would be a takeaway curry from the Taj Mahal in the high street – a fact his mum was well aware of. He might as well come clean.

'Josie,' he mumbled, his hand half-covering his mouth.

'Who, I didn't hear you?'

He could tell she'd heard perfectly well by the smirk on her face.

'Josie,' he repeated, louder this time.

She busied herself getting the ingredients out of various cupboards, and he felt a bit of a heel for stealing his parents' evening meal.

'I knew there was more to this dog sitting business than you were letting on,' she said. 'See, I told you Poppy would liven you up – she's got you a girlfriend!'

'Josie's not my girlfriend.'

His mother's look was sharp. 'But you want her to be, don't you?'

All Theo could do was to shake his head mutely.

'Righto, let's see if you can impress her with a portion of lamb shank. I'm going to show you how it's done – so watch and learn, sonny, watch and learn.'

CHAPTER 22

Day-old lamb shank tasted just as good as freshly-made lamb shank, Theo decided, as he licked the spoon clean. The concoction had been bubbling away in the oven for the past half hour, so should be well and truly heated through by now.

He checked the table again, wondering for the twentieth time if he should light a candle. His mum had given him a ruddy great big one to put on the mantelpiece, claiming that it would give the room a certain ambience. All Theo could think of was that it would give Josie the wrong impression. Candles equalled a date in an expensive restaurant in his opinion, and this evening was not a date. It was a meal between a couple of… what? He couldn't refer to Josie as a friend, considering he was paying her, but they seemed to have moved on from a simple business relationship. Besides, candles were meant to be lit when it was dark, and considering it was only seven-thirty on an August evening in the northern hemisphere, it was still light. So, no, no candles. Sorry, Mum.

When he heard Josie's knock, Theo took a deep breath and ran his hands through his hair. For some reason, his innards had gone all fluttery and his heart was doing a peculiar double-thump. He felt warm too, and hoped he wasn't coming down with anything; he didn't want to spend any part of what was left of his precious time off this summer being ill.

'Hi, come in,' he said, hastily opening the door, and feeling rather flustered. He wasn't used to entertaining, and he was worried that the carrots might boil dry, or the new potatoes would turn to mush if he wasn't there to hover over them. Perhaps he should have gone with the steak option? With several things cooking at once, he wasn't sure he could cope.

'Mmm, what are we having? It smells divine.' Josie sniffed the air appreciatively, as did Crumble until he was distracted by a bouncy Poppy.

The pair of them dashed off into the kitchen, with their owners following at a slightly more sedate pace.

'Lamb shank,' Theo squeaked, clearing his throat as nerves got the better of him. Sort yourself out, he muttered silently. He dealt with challenging kids as a profession – surely he could deal with one lovely young lady and her dog? He just needed to stop wondering that she might think this was a date, when it so clearly wasn't. In fact, his thinking about it was getting out of hand and he was in danger of over-thinking everything.

'I haven't had lamb for ages,' Josie said, and Theo had a sudden horrible thought that she might not like it.

'Um… you do like lamb? I mean, if you don't I could always—'

'I love lamb. I just don't eat it very often because it's so damned expensive.'

'Oh, good. That you like it, I mean, not that it's expensive.' And, just so she wouldn't think he was showing off on the meat front, he added, 'My mum gave it to me.'

Josie raised her eyebrows.

Oh dear, now he sounded like an idiot. 'I popped round to hers yesterday, and she was…' He stopped and pulled a face, not fancying having to explain that his mum had more or less forced him to learn to cook it.

'I'm sure it'll be delicious wherever it came from,' she said, putting a hand on his arm.

He'd noticed she tended to do that quite a lot, and he wished she wouldn't because it made him go all tingly. He didn't need to get tingly when Josie was around. He had needed to get tingly with Marie or

Robyn (*Robyn* – oh dear… he never should have kissed her), but he hadn't felt a thing.

'Take a seat,' he offered. 'All I've got to do is drain the veg and the potatoes and we're good to go. Fancy a glass of wine?'

'Just the one, thanks. I'll pour it.'

'Use this one,' he suggested, using a spoon to point to the already opened bottle – the rest of the contents had been used to make the sauce for the lamb.

'OK, I'll save this for next time,' she said, moving the bottle she'd brought with her out of the way and reaching for the opened one.

Next time?

Oh, my.

The very idea of there being a next time sent shivers right through him.

Crikey, what on earth was he doing?

And as the pair of them settled down to enjoy their meal, the two dogs gnawing on chews at their feet, he continued to ask himself the same question. Because he really, really liked her. More than liked her. The other women he'd been out with recently weren't a patch on her. Neither Marie nor Robyn made him feel the way Josie made him feel, and if he was totally honest, none of the women he'd been out with prior to them had made him feel like this, either.

He had to admit it – he was falling for Josie. If he

hadn't fallen already, that is.

And he wasn't sure what he should do about it.

Should he bite the bullet and go with the flow, or should he fight it?

'That was wonderful,' she said, placing her knife and fork neatly together on the plate and leaning back.

'I've got a confession,' Theo blurted.

'Go on…?' She didn't appear to be alarmed, and he had a feeling she knew exactly what he was about to say.

'My mother helped me make it.'

Josie bit her lip as she tried not to smile, and he noticed a cute dimple in each cheek that he hadn't spotted before.

Oh, God, she was simply adorable.

'I guessed she might have had a hand in it,' she said, a laugh finally escaping her lips.

Those lips, those luscious, pink lips…

Theo abruptly got to his feet and began clearing away the dishes. 'It's not that funny,' he said huffily, but his smile told her he hadn't taken any real offence. 'She offered, OK?'

'Or did you ask?'

He stacked the dirty plates next to the sink and leant against the counter. 'It was a bit of both.' He sucked in a deep breath. 'I'll be honest with you – I'm not the brilliant cook you think I am. The reason I called into my mum's yesterday was to borrow something from her freezer. Something she'd already made.'

'Like *Blue Peter*? Here's one I made earlier?' She mimed holding up a dish.

'Yeah… I can't really cook.'

'Did you make any of it?'

'I did! But with a lot of supervision,' he confessed.

'Your mother seems to be a good cook.'

'She is. I'll have to ask her to give me more lessons.'

'How about if you come to my house next time?'

There she was, talking about a next time again.

'Sounds great,' he said.

'Saturday? Unless you're busy, of course.'

Theo couldn't contain his smile. 'I'm not busy, so Saturday would be fantastic.' He turned back to the sink and ran the hot tap. Why, oh why had he just agreed to another meal? And at her house, too? He must be a glutton for punishment. Or stupid. Probably both.

'Let me help you with those, then how about we take the dogs for a walk?' she suggested. 'It's a lovely evening.'

It certainly was, he noticed, looking out of the kitchen window. And Poppy could do with a stroll. Not to mention, that he didn't want the evening to end just yet. 'We could always sit on the patio and open the other bottle of red?' he offered.

'Look.' Josie was pointing to her stomach.

Theo looked. It was a lovely stomach. Not totally flat, but with a tiny curve to it that he desperately wanted to run his finger over.

'I've got a food baby,' she continued. 'I'm going to have to exercise that off.'

'Eh?'

'Eaten too much. See?' She pointed again.

Theo saw, and he liked what he saw very much indeed. Her tummy was perfect.

He drew in a steadying breath and said, 'A walk around the park should see to that. Not that there is anything to see to,' he added hastily. 'You've got a lovely tummy… oh, dear. I'm sorry, I didn't mean—'

Josie was biting her lip again. 'That's OK, I don't mind being complimented on my stomach. In fact, I think that's the first time anyone has said anything nice about it.'

They both looked at the area in question. Theo swiftly looked away again, and caught her gazing at him with an amused expression.

'Have you been to Tyddesley Wood?' she asked.

'Not for years. I used to go there when I was a boy.' He remembered picnics in the wood, his mother being careful not to trample on the wild flowers growing here, while he and his dad built a den out of fallen branches. 'Is it OK to take Poppy? I've been worried about not walking her too far because she's so young.'

'We'll take the car, and have a short walk; although I'm sure Poppy will let you know when she's had enough and wants to be picked up.'

When they arrived at their destination, Theo had forgotten just how lovely the former deer park was. Long ago it had been owned by the Abbots of Pershore Abbey, but these days it was under the care of Worcestershire Wildlife Trust.

'I love coming here,' Josie said, as Theo parked the car and they got out, the dogs bounding ahead full of waggy-tailed joy. 'See those trees?' Theo glanced over to where she was pointing. 'That used to be an orchard years ago, and some of the trees still bear fruit, like plums, crab apples and pears. It dates back to the days when there used to be a thriving fruit-growing and market gardening industry here.'

Theo was impressed. He'd hardly ever looked at the trees, except to wonder which ones he could climb – which spoke volumes about the last time he visited the wood. He wouldn't dream of climbing a tree now!

It was cool beneath the canopy and the leaf cover overhead blocked out most of the setting sun, so it was more like twilight as they wound their way along well-trodden paths, the dogs following closely behind. Or in front. Sometimes to the sides. But where one was, the other wasn't far away. Theo couldn't decide whether Crumble was looking after the pup, or whether Poppy was too wary of this new place to risk wandering too far from the older dog's side.

Taking in a deep breath of the gloriously fresh air, Theo stopped and gazed around. 'I'd forgotten how beautiful a woodland could be,' he said. 'Or maybe I'd never noticed in the first place. Too busy being a kid, I expect.'

'Soul food,' Josie said. 'Places like this one feed the soul. I never fail to come back from a walk like this without feeling refreshed and revitalised and glad to be alive. There's definitely something to be said for getting back to nature, and simply *being*. I love not seeing another person – you don't count,' she added generously, nudging his arm with her elbow. 'There's nothing manmade in sight, although the woodland is carefully managed to protect all the wonderful species of plants and animals that live here.'

'I think I'm going to make this one of my regular places to walk Poppy when she's a bit older.' He thought the pup might be starting to flag, as she was spending increasing amounts of time nearer to him and not chasing after the awfully energetic spaniel. Once or twice he'd felt a paw on his leg, as she asked to be picked up. He'd give her a little while longer, to ensure she was worn out before he gave in to her demands and carried her.

'There are so many other wonderful places nearby,' Josie told him. 'Piddle Brook Meadows, Humpy Meadow, Grafton Wood... That's the fantastic thing about owning a dog – getting out and about. Because if you don't exercise them, they tend to get naughty and cranky. You can't not take your dog out, not unless you don't mind them taking your house apart.'

'I'm even looking forward to the winter,' Theo admitted, scooping Poppy up and letting her snuggle her nose into his neck. The tickle of her breath on his skin made him chuckle.

The light was starting to leave the sky by the time they headed back to the car, and it was getting rather dark in the wood itself. But as they stepped out from under the trees and into a meadow, Theo looked up to see the sky painted in shades of orange, pink, and purple. He didn't think he'd seen anything so beautiful...

Until he glanced at Josie.

Her skin was illuminated by the last rays of the sun, and her hair shone and shimmered as she took in the glorious scene. Her eyes glimmered, large and luminous, and he couldn't stop staring at her.

'It's beautiful,' she said softly.

'Yes, it is,' he agreed, his eyes never leaving her face. Not even when she brought her attention to him and saw that he was talking about her, and not the sunset.

She cocked her head slightly, questioning, her expression solemn, and without thinking about what he was doing he took a step towards her and slowly lowered the tired pup to the ground, not taking his gaze off her.

When he straightened up, she caught her bottom lip between her teeth and her eyes widened.

Not caring any more about whether he was doing the best thing, he let out a small cry and gathered her to him, feeling her melt into his embrace as his arms came around her, holding her so tightly he was worried he might hurt her.

But when he pulled back a little, she snaked her own arms around his neck and stood on tiptoe. Was she really so tiny? He hadn't realised how small and delicate she was, how much taller than her he was. And the way she slotted into his arms like she was made for just that purpose, sent a wave of desire and protectiveness through him. He wanted her so badly it hurt. But more than that, he wanted to keep her safe, to care for her, to cherish her.

Far too late to stop, far too late to consider what he was doing, he bent his head to hers and sought her lips, and his last sight of her for several long minutes as his mouth claimed hers, was of her long lashes lying against her cheek and the flush of colour on her skin.

As he breathed the sweet, fresh scent of her

perfume (or was that *her*?), his senses reeled and he pulled her even more tightly to him, sinking into the kiss until he was completely lost to her soft lips, her gentle breath, the way she felt in his arms, her curves, her foot nudging his leg—

Poppy.

He felt the dog's cold wet nose through the fabric of his jeans, and oh so reluctantly he ended the embrace, his mouth withdrawing from Josie's in a series of fluttering kisses, until he was resting his forehead against hers and trying to control his breathing.

'Wow.' It was so softly spoken, Theo wondered if he'd actually heard Josie say the word, or whether he'd imagined it.

'Wow,' she repeated again, a fraction louder and, unable to resist, he found her mouth again. This time when her lips parted, he let out a small cry of his own as the sheer delight of kissing her swept him away.

Another nudge, followed by a pair of scrabbling paws as the puppy brought him back to himself, ended the second even more wonderful kiss and he sighed with amused reluctance as he was forced to set Josie free from his encircling arms.

Josie appeared to have other ideas, and she kept hers firmly around his neck until an annoyed yip made her giggle and step back.

Theo was suddenly overcome with shyness and he bent down to retrieve his dog, too scared to see Josie's face. From the way she'd acted, she had appeared to enjoy the kiss as much as he'd done, but what he didn't want was for it to have been a fleeting thing which didn't mean anything to her. Because it had meant a great deal to him. A very great deal, indeed.

Josie broke the silence. 'It's a magical night,' she said, her face lifted to the sky, and when he looked at her he realised she was right, it *was* magical, but he didn't mean the rapidly-darkening night – he meant *her*, and the kiss they had just shared.

CHAPTER 23

It was official – Theo wanted to date Josie. After that kiss he wanted to spend every waking moment with her, and the ones where he was asleep, too. Never had he felt like this about anyone, ever. It was rather disconcerting he must admit, but exhilaratingly, heart-poundingly wonderful at the same time.

What he also wanted to do was to woo her properly (what a lovely old-fashioned word "woo" was, and it described how he felt perfectly) and do something without the dogs. Unfortunately, he had little idea whether she'd like to go to the cinema, the theatre, an art gallery (he wasn't too keen on those), a meal in a nice restaurant… And if he did suggest the theatre, he had no clue as to the types of plays she liked; the same thing applied to the cinema. He supposed he could let her choose, but where was the romance in that? He wanted to whisk her off her feet by presenting her with a fait accompli, where he'd thought of every little detail and had left nothing to chance.

But what if he was going a bit too fast for her? A couple of kisses was all they'd shared, and there he was, diving in feet first and assuming she'd want an all-out relationship.

What if he took things a little easier, and suggested something that was half date and half puppy stuff? He knew she liked to read because there were loads of books in her living room – maybe they could go to a coffee shop inside a book shop which allowed dogs in? He remembered seeing one advertised ages ago, and at the time he'd wondered whether dogs and books were a good mix. Now, however, he came to the conclusion that it was a perfect mix, made even more perfect by the addition of coffee and cake.

He was about to meet her in the park on the tail end of one of her long walks with a couple of her other charges, so that Poppy could get used to being walked alongside them, and his heart was doing its ridiculous pounding thing whenever he thought of her. Which was all the time, so he was seriously worried that he might need to see a doctor if he kept this up.

Spotting her in the distance with Crumble and three other dogs at her heels, his mouth went dry and the palms of his hands became damp.

Crikey, he was a right old mess, and if this is what

love felt like then he wasn't sure he wanted any part of it.

Hang on, did he just think the "L" word?

Oh…

Having never been in love before, he wasn't sure he knew what the signs or the symptoms were, and there was no time to look them up now because she was walking towards him with a smile on her face and laughter in her eyes.

God, she was gorgeous! His heart skipped a beat and his stomach did a weird somersault that made him feel slightly sick and all gooey at the same time.

He watched her approach, her charges following obediently. She was totally at home with the dogs, and he marvelled at the way she was able to effortlessly control four dogs at once. He could barely manage one, although Poppy was being a sweetheart and sitting quietly at his feet while she waited for the newcomers to approach. Crumble gave her a welcoming sniff and a lick across her face, and the other three made their introductions in the usual canine way.

Theo let Poppy deal with it by herself; he knew Josie wouldn't tolerate any poor behaviour from any of the pooches she looked after, and he was content to stare into her wonderful eyes instead.

They were shining back at him, and he fell right in, losing himself in their depths.

'Earth to Theo,' she giggled and he came to with a start.

'Sorry, I was miles away,' he said, hoping she didn't think he was strange.

'Where did you go?' she asked softly.

Into your soul, he wanted to say, and it was beautiful. 'Fancy a coffee?'

'Now?' She reached down to tickle Poppy behind her ears.

'Not right now. I was thinking after you've taken the other dogs home. I know a book shop with a café in it that allows dogs in.'

'Sounds perfect – my favourite three things, coffee, cake and canines.' She turned her attention from the animals to him. 'Four favourite things,' she amended, her pupils large, her lips slightly apart.

Oh God, she was flirting with him, and it made him go all weak at the knees. Weak in the head, too, he thought after blurting, 'I love cake. And coffee. Dogs are good, too.'

'I'll look forward to it. I might even treat myself to a new book. You can't beat a proper paperback, can you?'

She was letting him off the hook, and he breathed out slowly trying to persuade his heart to resume its usual steady rhythm and not try to jump out of his chest.

'What sort of books do you like? he asked, feeling on safer ground.

'Romances. The spicier the better.' She shot him a mischievous look, and his cheeks grew warm.

He wanted to fan himself. Or have a cold shower…

'Joking. I like horror,' she amended.

'You do? Have you read any of Ben Cheetham's?'

'I have!' she cried and he breathed a sigh of relief that they had something other than their dogs in common.

Josie was quite widely-read, he discovered, as they sauntered around the park discussing books they'd read.

'I beg to differ,' she was saying after he'd teased her about her love of Emily Brontë. 'Have you even *read* it? Wuthering Heights is *not* a romance – a love story, yes, but not a romance. And it's awfully creepy in parts and full of dark suspense.'

'It sounds intriguing, and no I haven't read it. I just assumed it was a romance. Do you like it because it's dark or because it's a love story?'

'Both I suppose, but mainly because of the passion in it – all that destructive love that survives beyond death, is wonderful and awful at the same time.'

Her own passion for the story and for her love of literature as a whole, made him feel all hot and bothered.

'How about films?' he asked to change the subject.

'I don't watch many, and I can't remember the last time I went to the cinema. I prefer watching documentaries.'

Theo's heart sank. His staple evening viewing was a diet of box sets and series like The Walking Dead and Game of Thrones, both of which he'd seen about three times each. He was definitely a creature of habit. From what she'd just said, he couldn't imagine being cuddled up on the sofa together, because they wouldn't be able to agree on anything to watch.

This getting to know someone malarkey was hard, he thought. Were couples supposed to have loads in common, or was it true that opposites attract? Not that they were a couple as yet, but he sincerely hoped they might be.

Bugger it; he'd learn to like The History Channel and Eden if it meant spending time with Josie. And to be honest, he was hoping that the cuddling on the sofa would involve less watching and more cuddling...

He felt himself grow warm again. A cold shower would most certainly be in order when he got back! And if he wanted to save on his water bill, then he should try not to have such thoughts about her. But how could he not, when she was so gorgeous? Not only was she beautiful, but she was full of life and laughter, and he was drawn to her with all the inevitability of a moth to a flame. Is this what his mum meant when she'd said he needed livening up a bit?

His life was certainly livelier now Josie was in it. And Poppy. With half of his attention on the dog and the other half on Josie, he marvelled at how much his life had changed in a month. By letting a small, defenceless, cute (and Poppy was very cute indeed) puppy into his heart, he'd opened himself up to loving the most wonderful woman he'd ever met.

One by one they dropped off the dogs in Josie's care at their respective houses. Theo waiting patiently outside with Poppy, Crumble and those pooches who had yet to be taken home, until eventually it was just the two of them and their own dogs left.

'Shall we try that coffee-cum-book shop I mentioned, or do you have other plans?' he asked.

'A book shop that sells coffee sounds grand,' she said, slipping her arm through his as they made their way there.

The place didn't disappoint either; the dogs were made more welcome than their humans, and after hot drinks and gooey cake (the pooches were given home-made doggy biscuits, much to their delight), Theo remained at the table while Josie browsed the shelves.

'Aw, they're so cute, especially this little one,' a voice in his ear said, and Theo snapped out of studying Josie to find an elderly lady and her equally elderly husband cooing over the two animals. Crumble hadn't taken his eyes of his mistress (much like Theo) and wasn't paying any attention to the elderly couple, but Poppy was rolling around on the floor with her paws in the air, inviting these lovely new people to stroke her soft tummy.

'She's adorable,' the lady said, and for a second Theo thought she was referring to Josie, because she looked especially sweet when she was concentrating, her expression both serious and avid at the same time.

He ran through his stock answers, and after more petting and more cooing, the couple left just as Josie returned with her purchases.

Once they were outside, she said halted and fished around in the paper bag. 'This is for you,' she said, handing him a copy of Wuthering Heights.

Theo took it and laughed, delighted that she'd thought of him. 'Thank you! You shouldn't have.'

'I most certainly should have. You need educating.'

'In what? Love?' He'd said it before he had a chance to censor himself, and he groaned inwardly.

Josie moved closer, her body almost touching his, and he could have sworn he could feel the warmth of her skin as her perfume wafted over him. Her gaze was intense, and so deep he thought he was about to drown.

'I don't think you need any lessons in that subject,'

she breathed, and stretched up to kiss him, and once again he was lost to her, all coherent thought fled as he surrendered to the emotions surging through him.

Someone coughed and Theo remembered that they were in the middle of a pavement with shoppers all around them, and he ended the kiss reluctantly. As they broke apart, Josie giggled, a sound of pure happiness, and he couldn't help but join in.

'Look at us,' she chortled, 'acting like a couple of teenagers. What will people think?'

'I don't care. And just to show you how much I don't care, I'm going to do that again. May I?'

'You most certainly may.'

So he did. Very thoroughly, too!

CHAPTER 24

Theo felt like a parent who was on a sneaky night out without the kids. It was a strange feeling, as if he was doing something wrong. Poppy had certainly made him aware of her dismay that he was going out without her. She'd given him a massive dose of puppy dog eyes and a huge guilt trip as he closed the kitchen door on her and set off to pick Josie up.

They were going on a proper grown up date, without the dogs, just the two of them, and he was so excited he could pop.

He loved Poppy dearly, but the thought of having Josie all to himself was making his heart race. The fact that there'd be other people in the restaurant was neither here nor there; he'd left his responsibilities in the cottage for a couple of hours and he could focus all his attention on Josie tonight. And he couldn't wait!

'Wow, just wow!' he exclaimed as she opened her

door to his knock.

He'd never seen her looking so lovely and she took his breath away. Her hair floated around her face in a dark cloud, she was wearing lipstick (he found himself looking forward to kissing it off), and she was also wearing a dress – the first one he'd seen her in.

'Do I scrub up OK?' she asked.

'You look beautiful,' he breathed, and was rewarded with a brilliant smile.

'Thank you, kind sir. I thought I'd better make an effort.'

'You needn't have – you're beautiful anyway,' he replied, and he wasn't simply being gallant; he meant it. She was gorgeous and he was so lucky that she seemed to like him, too. He couldn't believe that such a lovely creature had agreed to go out with him and he kept wanting to pinch himself to check she was real.

He had chosen a restaurant with a good reputation, wanting to spoil her, guessing that money might be a bit tight for her. Although her dog caring business was thriving, he didn't think she earned a great deal. He got the impression she was frugal and that she enjoyed the simpler things in life, but tonight he wanted to treat her and to make her feel special.

The Woodman's was on the other side of Worcester, in a little village arching the River Severn. Not only was the restaurant renowned for its food, but the location and the ambience was pretty good too, so he'd been told. When he'd asked for recommendations on *Don't Tell the Missus*, Jenson had suggested it. After demanding to know why of course! The fact that he was taking a woman on a date had been a source of much teasing, all of it good-natured, and his mates were even more impressed when he'd informed them that he'd had a couple of dates with other women before Josie. Jenson had immediately cottoned on to Poppy being responsible for his sudden popularity, and he'd been forced to come clean. What he hadn't shared with them though, were his feelings for Josie. His emotions were too new and too fragile to be subjected to their harsh (though well meaning) banter. He knew they'd be delighted for him, but he wanted to keep it to himself until he was sure of his relationship with her. It was early days yet, and they were only just getting to know each other, and although he knew how he felt about her, he wasn't entirely sure she felt the same way about him. He hoped she did…

'It's lovely! Josie exclaimed, as he opened the door to the restaurant and ushered her inside, and he had to admit, she was right.

He'd been expecting more of a country-style theme, and although the outside of the building was typical old-worlde English charm, on the inside it was the total opposite. The restaurant was open plan, stretching the whole width of the pub, with floor to ceiling windows along the far wall, making the most of the fabulous views of the sleepy river and the muted purples of the Malvern Hills in the distance. Swans paddled majestically on the river and willow trees trailed their drooping branches in the water. The late evening sun streamed through the glass, bathing the room in a golden glow.

They were shown to a table near one of the windows and Theo felt as though they were sitting outside, especially since the chairs were angled away from the room so the only thing in his line of vision was the view – and Josie herself.

He knew which he preferred to stare at, and although he was extremely grateful that they'd been seated at one of the best tables in the place, he kept his attention on her lovely face.

Josie, after drinking in the view, twisted around to get a better look at the restaurant itself. 'It's trendier than I expected,' she said. 'I never did go for horse brasses and chintz.'

He craned his neck. There wasn't an inch of chintz in sight. But he noticed that every table was made out of a tree trunk, and that the chair he was sitting on appeared to be carved from a single piece of wood. They all were, each one individual and organic. Apart from the wood, white and green were the only other colours to be seen, the white being provided by the walls and the tablecloths, the green being provided by an array of plants – it was like dining in a forest clearing.

Josie had a huge smile on her face as she was staring around the room in wonder, so he guessed he'd made a good choice. Thanks, Jenson, he thought; I owe you one. He just hoped the food was as impressive.

The menu certainly looked good, and the pair of them were spoilt for choice.

'Have a starter,' Theo urged, his mouth watering at the delicious smells filling the air. He seriously wanted to try everything and was having difficulty deciding.

'I'll have the salt-cured salmon with blood orange and fennel, to start,' Josie said to the hovering waiter, 'and grilled buttermilk chicken with spicy nduja sauce and rainbow chard for the main course.'

Theo settled on ricotta with chilli and peppers, and roast duck with grilled cabbage and blood orange marmalade. After the waiter had taken their order and glided away, Theo joked, 'I think they must have a glut of blood oranges, and what is nduja sauce anyway?'

'No idea, but I guess we'll soon find out,' she laughed.

They chatted about the dogs for a while (of course) and Theo marvelled at how easy she was to talk to. They were on the same wavelength and even when there was a brief lull in the conversation, it was a companionable silence.

'Do you fancy sharing?' she asked when their starters arrived. 'See, this is why I don't eat out very often – I order something, then fancy a bit of whatever is on the other person's plate.'

'We can swap if you like.'

'But I want to eat mine, too,' she wailed. 'It looks so yummy.'

In the end, they went halfsies, and Theo popped a good portion of his ricotta onto her plate, receiving a wedge of salmon in return.

'Mmm,' she said, taking a mouthful of the fish and squinting at him in bliss. 'This is divine.'

He had to agree, but he had a feeling he was referring to her rather than to the food, which he barely tasted.

They shared their main courses too, to the silent amusement of their waiter, who appeared now and again to top up Josie's wine glass or to ask if Theo needed any more sparkling water. By the time they ordered dessert, the kitchen had realised what they were up to and had put a portion of each pudding on the two plates, causing Josie to dissolve in a fit of giggles.

'I've had too much wine,' she declared, her giggles turning into hiccups. 'I'm not used to it.'

'Maybe a couple of coffees might be a good idea?'

Josie nodded, and while they waited for their drinks she gazed out of the window. Dusk had fallen and uplights now illuminated the grounds of the restaurant and tiny fairy lights were strung in the trees, but the charm of it all was practically lost on Theo as he spent the time surreptitiously watching the woman he was with.

Without meaning to, he let out a sigh; she was lovely, incredibly lovely and—

'I know you're itching to do it,' she said, breaking into his thoughts, 'so go ahead, I don't mind.'

'I'm sorry... do what?' Could she honestly tell that he wanted to kiss her?

'Check on Poppy. Isn't that why you're looking so wistful? I'm sure she's fine, but you won't rest until you know she's OK.'

'Oh, yes, Poppy.' Theo hadn't forgotten about the pup exactly, but she hadn't been at the forefront of his mind, either.

'Ah, look at her,' he said, after a few moments spent peering at his phone. He showed Josie. The dog was asleep in her basket, curled into a tight ball which was her favourite position when Theo wasn't around for her to cuddle up with. 'She won't sleep tonight, though,' he added, grimacing.

'It does get better, you know.' Then she burst out

laughing 'It sounds like we're talking about a child, not a puppy.'

'I know which I'd prefer,' Theo muttered, then went on to explain about Jenson and his impending fatherhood.

'Do you ever want children?' she asked.

He thought carefully about the answer. 'One day, with the right woman.'

'I would have thought teaching the little darlings might have put you off.'

'Not really, although eight years in the profession can make you a bit jaded.'

'Is that what's happened to you?'

'I suppose. Teaching can be a thankless task sometimes, but when you see a kid finally grasp a concept or work a problem out for themselves and see the way their eyes light up, then it makes it all worthwhile. Sort of.' He paused. 'I used to love my job, I used to love teaching, but now I don't think my heart is in it anymore. Even in the short time that I've been teaching, the profession has changed. And not for the better, either.'

'But schools need people like you. The children do, too.'

Theo laughed. 'That's nice of you to say so, but I might be an awful teacher for all you know.'

'I bet you aren't. I can tell you care about your

pupils.'

'The way you could tell I'd fallen in love with Poppy?'

Josie shrugged. 'It's a gift, what can I say?' Pushing her empty coffee cup away, she got to her feet. 'Let's go,' she said. 'You've left that little floof on her own for long enough.'

'Oh, but it's not that late,' he protested, not wanting the evening to end just yet.

'It's not, is it? Shall we go back to yours?'

'Both of us? What about Crumble?'

'He'll be fine for another hour or so.' She gave him a little wink, and his stomach did a triple backflip.

Just the thought of being alone with her made his heart pound, and if an hour was all he was going to get to kiss her senseless, then he'd accept it gladly.

CHAPTER 25

Theo could hardly believe that almost five out of the six weeks summer hols had already gone. The time had flown by and his heart had sunk to his trainers when he'd realised that tomorrow was GCSE results day.

He should go into school but he seriously didn't want to, and it wasn't only because he'd have to leave Poppy on her own for a couple of hours. OK, that was the main reason, but the other was that he wasn't sure he could face going into work before he absolutely had to. The teacher training day in September would be soon enough to be told that his grades were down, or that he hadn't hit his target. Not that it had ever happened in the past, but there was always a first time, and this year he'd advised against entering the whole of Year 10 for their maths exam early because only the top set was anywhere near ready. It was going to be a gamble as to whether 10.3 (soon to be 11.3) would be ready next year, let alone this, so he was dreading seeing their results.

But he'd better go in. It would look bad if he didn't. Whatever he thought about Year 10, it was the current Year 11 pupils who'd need his support and advice now, and he couldn't let them down.

With leaden boots (he was actually wearing pristine trainers) he got ready for work, deciding at the last minute to take Poppy with him.

The pup danced around his feet as he attempted to wrestle her harness over her head, and her antics soon cheered him up as she hopped onto the passenger seat and waited to be strapped in, gazing at him expectantly.

'You won't like it,' he told her, but all he got was a wet kiss on his nose as he reached across her to fasten her doggy seat belt (who knew such things existed?).

Actually, that wasn't true – the pup liked being anywhere so long as either he or Josie was there too. Even Crumble would do at a push, because in her eyes anything was better than being shut in the kitchen on her own. As usual, she curled up on the seat and waited patiently to be driven to wherever it was they were going, simply content to be in his company. And Theo was equally as content to be in hers.

The thought of having to leave her once the new academic year started filled him with dismay. He knew she'd be exceedingly well looked after by Josie (who was now going to have her all day, instead of popping in to take the pup for a walk), but he had a feeling he was going to miss her dreadfully.

Nearly as much as he was going to miss Josie, in fact. Since their meal at the Woodsman they had practically been inseparable, spending most of the day together and a decent chunk of the evening, too, only parting to go home to their respective beds.

Theo desperately wanted to get her into his (or him into hers – he wasn't fussy about the location) but he also wanted to take it slowly and not rush into something they might regret. As things stood, it was fun getting to know her and he was happy (ish) to wait.

As he pulled into his favourite space, he realised from the scarcity of cars in the car park that he was quite early, and he shook his head, smiling. Poppy had altered his sleeping patterns so much so that he couldn't stay in bed past six-thirty in the morning even if he wanted to.

The school was open though, the caretaker having arrived at his usual seven a.m. and the head teacher's parking space was occupied. He recognised one or two of the other vehicles, and there were a few parents sitting in cars with their respective offspring, waiting for the official time to collect their results.

Theo gave a half-hearted wave or two to the children he recognised as he and Poppy scuttled inside, where he headed straight for the maths department office. As he suspected, his head of department hadn't arrived yet, so he took it upon himself to check the print out of figures.

Not bad, he decided, as he scrolled down the list of pupils' names and their corresponding results. As usual, there were a few surprises – both good and bad, but all in all, the results were as predicted. Theo was pleased to see that his own classes had performed particularly well and he relaxed enough to make a coffee, which he drank before heading off to the main hall for the usual results day drama.

'Is this yours?'

Theo heard the head teacher's voice and he slowed his pace to allow Mr Fitzpatrick to catch up. 'Sorry, I didn't want to leave her on her own, and I really wanted to be here for the children.' It was kind of true; more true now that he'd seen the results for himself than it had been earlier.

'Didn't know you had a dog,' Mr Fitzpatrick stated, bending down to ruffle Poppy's head. Poppy licked his hand and he smiled. 'He's nice, isn't he?'

'I think so.'

'Hard work, though, and a bit of a tie,' the head teacher added, and Theo was tempted to point out that a dog was considerably less work and less of a tie than a child was, but he held his tongue. Mr Fitzpatrick had five, and if that wasn't the epitome of hard work, then Theo didn't know what was.

'Can't just go for a weekend away when you've got animals to consider,' Mr Fitzpatrick added, and Theo bit back a grin. He didn't think an impromptu few days away would be all that easy to organise when you had a handful of kids either. And to be fair, Theo hadn't had all that many spontaneous weekends away prior to acquiring Poppy, so he didn't feel the lack. Besides, he'd discovered that with a bit of research it was possible to find places that would allow well-behaved dogs in, so it wasn't all bad.

'Your department did all right,' the head teacher continued as they walked down the corridor to the hall, where Theo could hear the buzz of voices.

'I saw.'

'You did good. There are a couple of eyebrow raisers, but that happens every year. Take Emmett Young, for instance. Who'd have thought he'd do so well? Ah, I see the hordes have already arrived. Right then, into the fray.' The head teacher squared his shoulders and rolled his neck as if he was about to step into battle, then he was off, shaking hands and exclaiming over results, leaving Theo and Poppy staring after him, bemused. Theo was the one who was bemused, that is; Poppy was spoilt for choice as to who to wag her tail at first. She was such a friendly little thing.

'Awright?'

Theo blinked when he saw who had spoken. 'You're early, Tim.' Tim Hogan never arrived at school before nine-thirty and always had an array of excuses handy as to why he was late. Theo's favourite was that Edmund Styles had kipped at their house and Tim had wanted to eat breakfast with him before he left. Edmund Styles, the famous footballer? Yeah, as if that had happened… Still, ten out of ten for imagination – even though the score was nil for believability.

'It's my mum, innit? She told me I had to come.'

'Is she here?' Theo glanced around the hall.

'Nah, did a late shift in the club, didn't she? She'll be snoring her head off.'

Tim didn't paint a particularly pleasant picture of his mother, but Theo knew for a fact that the woman held down two jobs while caring for three children. 'At least you're here. How did you do?' Theo hadn't looked at the Year 10 results yet, having been more interested in those all-important Year 11 figures; they were the ones that the school was judged on and the ones which the Local Authority would hold them accountable for.

'OK, I s'pose.' He thrust an already dirty and crumpled piece of paper at Theo and while Theo scanned it, he crouched down to stroke Poppy.

Theo read the results twice, and a smile broke out

on his face. For a pupil who had been predicted to achieve poor grades, he'd managed a 4 in maths and a 5 in English. Theo was surprised, as he'd predicted a 2 for the boy. 'You did extremely well in your maths,' he said. 'Well done! I knew you could do it.'

Tim straightened up and looked Theo in the eye. Theo was disconcerted to realise that Tim was almost as tall as him. When had that happened?

'I can do better, Mr Martin. I know I can. I'm gonna, next year.'

'You are? You want to take your maths again?'

'And my English. My Mum says I have to.'

'I thought your mother was in bed.'

'She was. I rang her and told her.'

'I bet she was pleased.'

'Yeah, but she said I can do better.'

Theo nodded slowly and thoughtfully. 'She's right, you can. I'll be honest with you, I didn't think you'd get more than a 2.'

Tim gave him a level stare. 'I know. Shocked you, didn't I?'

'Not because you're not capable – you are – but because you don't give a monkey's uncle about school.'

Tim shrugged. 'It's boring.'

'Do you think work will be any more exciting?'

Another shrug. 'I'll get paid for it though, won't I?'

'Minimum wage, that's all'

'Not if I work for myself.'

'Doing what?'

'I dunno… Plumbing? Building? I'm gonna run my own business.'

'You'll need to be able to cost out jobs, prepare quotes, converse with clients, keep a record of accounts, pay VAT, tax, wages… the list is endless. And school might be boring, but it'll give you the groundwork to be able to do all that.'

Tim scuffed his foot on the floor. 'I know all this, don't I? That's why I said I can do better.'

'Saying it is one thing; meaning it, and doing it are different things entirely.'

Another shrug, but Theo felt as though he was finally getting through to the boy. The results had helped, enabling the pupil to see for himself what he might be capable of.

'So, are you going to come to school next year, or are you going to skive as much as you did in Year 10?' Theo asked.

Tim grinned. 'Might do. I did all right this year without all having to sit in boring lessons every day.'

'You'll do even better if you show up more than twice a week,' Theo pointed out.

There was silence for a moment. Tim's attention was on Poppy, who was sitting as his feet and looking up at him with her liquid brown eyes.

When Tim finally turned his attention to Theo, there was something in the careworn teenager's eyes what hadn't been there before.

Hope.

'Promise?' the boy asked.

'I promise. I'll do everything I can to help you get a better result. But you've got to promise to do your part, too. This is *your* future, Tim, not mine, and you've got to take responsibility for it, because no one else will.'

'Shit, man, that's a bit deep for a Thursday morning, innit?'

'Don't swear,' Theo replied automatically, but he was smiling and so was Tim, and Theo made a silent vow to himself that he wouldn't let this kid down. He didn't want to let any of them down. They all deserved the best he could give them, even if they didn't want it and didn't appreciate it.

'Mr Martin?'

'Yes, Tim?'

'Can you bring your dog to school every day, because she's, like, way cooler than you are.'

And with that, the boy sauntered off, with a teenage swagger and a couple of high-fives to some of the older boys on the way, leaving Theo with a smile on his face and a warm feeling in his chest.

CHAPTER 26

Theo groaned and pulled his dead arm out from underneath Josie. 'I'm going to have to get some work done tomorrow,' he said.

'Like what? I thought you teacher types had six weeks of lounging about.' She sat up and glanced at the time. 'I'd better be off. I've got ten dogs who need walking in the morning.'

'Not all at once, surely?'

'I'm good, but not that good. I'll do them in batches.'

'Phew. For a moment, I imagined all those dogs dragging you halfway across the county.'

Josie narrowed her eyes at him. 'Just how daft do you think I am? No, don't answer that. But you can answer my earlier question. What work?'

'Planning, lesson preparation, data analysis.' He sighed dramatically. 'I'd better get started tomorrow, or else the start of term will be here before I know it.'

'Don't take this the wrong way, but I get the feeling you're not entirely enamoured about going back to school.'

Theo thought for a moment. 'I didn't think I was either, but now I'm not so sure.' He gave a small, sad smile. 'When I first started out, I had visions of being a guiding influence on young minds, shaping my pupils; I don't know… being a cross between Goodbye Mr Chips and Dead Poets Society. Lately though, I'm beginning to think I'm more like a male version of Cameron Diaz in Bad Teacher. Not as good-looking, obviously. And my goal isn't to buy new boobs.'

'You certainly do like your films, don't you?' Josie said, smiling up at him from her position curled against his chest.

'It's sad, I know, but until you and Poppy came into my life, I didn't do much except work, sleep, and watch stuff on the TV in between.'

'What about your friends on the WhatsApp chat?'

'They're either seriously dating, married, married with a baby on the way, married and already have kids. I'm the odd one out, except for Chris who is divorced and lives in Ireland, and we don't hear from him often.'

She stretched up to kiss him on the cheek. 'I don't think you're odd. I also think you're just as good looking as Cameron Diaz.'

'Flatterer,' he murmured, cupping her face and dipping his head until his mouth was inches away from hers. 'I'm not the odd one out anymore.' He hesitated. 'Am I?'

'You most certainly are not,' she replied softly. 'Now stop messing about and kiss me.'

He did so, with considerable enthusiasm.

It was with considerably less eagerness that he eventually released her. 'I'll walk you back,' he stated, his heart still pounding and his head still spinning. She drove him crazy, in a nice way. He couldn't get enough of her, and he knew that as soon as they said goodbye he'd be counting the hours until he saw her again.

As they walked slowly along the lane, his hand in hers, the dogs trotting cheerfully beside them, Theo thought he'd never felt as happy. He hadn't realised just how empty and lacking his life had been before first Poppy and then Josie had come into it. He wasn't entirely sure he was any livelier than he had been before his mum had dumped a dog on him, but he was undoubtedly more contented. He felt more alive than he had done in years possibly not since his student days when he was young and carefree and he felt as though he had the whole world at his feet.

Gradually the youthful joy had eroded until he'd become stale and jaded, and fairly cynical about life in general. It hadn't helped that all his friends had found love and had settled down, leaving him to his lonely, unfulfilled bachelorhood.

Now though, he'd rediscovered his zest for life.

And he'd also found love.

He wondered if he should tell Josie how he felt about her. Or was it too soon? They'd only known each other just over a month, although it seemed like he'd known her forever, and he couldn't remember what his life had been like before she'd come into it.

He decided against saying anything just yet, even though he desperately wanted to tell her how he felt, because he was worried about scaring her off. She clearly liked him, else she wouldn't be with him, but he didn't know how deep her feelings went, and he was terrified that if she didn't feel as strongly about him as he did about her, it might break his heart.

No, best not to say anything yet. There was plenty of time. He'd let their relationship grow a little more before he told her he loved her.

His phone pinged. Then pinged again, and before he'd taken another couple of steps, it was pinging incessantly.

There was something happening on the group chat and, with an apologetic look at Josie, he pulled the gadget from his pocket and checked his messages, hoping it wasn't anything bad.

'Well I never!' he exclaimed, coming to a sudden

stop.

'Is everything all right?'

'Bella has had the baby. It's a little girl and mum and daughter are doing fine,' he read. 'It looks like she was a couple of weeks early, but she's healthy. I'll just congratulate Jenson and his wife. Won't be a tick.' He began typing furiously, a big grin on his face.

'That's wonderful news,' Josie said. 'I love babies.'

'I'll have to take you to see her. Once they're home from hospital, of course. Seven pounds three ounces. Is that good?'

'It's a decent size. Have they got a name for her, yet?'

'No idea,' he replied. 'Jenson hasn't mentioned one. I hope she looks like her mother, and not her father. Hang on, I've got to tell him that.'

'Men,' Josie grumbled, but she was smiling too. 'I bet you can't wait to give her a cuddle.'

Theo looked up from his phone, horrified. 'Not a chance! She's a *baby*! I might drop her or something.'

'I'm sure you won't. You'll be great.'

He shook his head. 'I won't be. Little ones, especially babies, scare me. Why do you think I teach eleven-year-olds and upwards?'

Her gaze met his and his heart flipped over. 'I bet you'll make a wonderful father, one day.'

'Really?' he squeaked, and hastily cleared his throat.

'Really. I've seen the way you are with Poppy.'

She was standing so close he could feel the warmth of her. 'Poppy's a dog,' he pointed out. 'Different thing entirely.'

'Is it? Go on, admit it, you love her – almost as much as a father loves his child.'

'Or a man loves a woman…?'

'Yes…' Her voice was dreamy and breathy, her lips were pink and soft, and her expression took his breath away. There was love in her eyes, and in that instant he knew she felt the same way about him as he did about her.

'The way this man loves you?' he asked, his voice hoarse, his throat dry. He was certain she must be able to hear the thud of his heart and she must assuredly be able to tell that he was trembling.

The rest of his life hung on this one moment. His future happiness hinged on her response.

'I hope so,' she whispered. 'Because I love you.'

His heart stopped. The whole world stopped. Time was frozen as he digested what she'd said.

She loved him? Her face told him the truth of it. No one could look at another person the way she was looking at him and not mean it.

She. Loved. Him.

Sheer joy swept through him, and he picked her up and spun her around, laughing loudly. 'I love you, too,' he cried at the top of his voice. 'I love you, I love you, *I love you*!'

Josie giggled, clinging to him for dear life as he whirled in a circle, her feet off the ground and her hair flying out behind her.

'Did you hear that, Poppy? Crumble? She loves me!' he cried.

Crumble barked and the two dogs bounced around them, jumping up in excitement.

'Put me down,' Josie cried. 'You're making me dizzy.'

Theo slowed and placed her gently on her feet. 'I've been dizzy from the first moment I saw you,' he said. 'I love you, Josie, and you've made me the happiest man in the world.'

He didn't know how long he stood in the lane kissing her, with the dogs at their feet and the stars wheeling overhead, but one thing he did know was that however long, it wasn't long enough. He intended to spend the rest of his life kissing this beautiful, remarkable woman, and even then it still wouldn't be long enough.

CHAPTER 27

Is that still a thing? Theo asked on the *Don't Tell the Missus* group chat.

Jenson: *I don't care if it isn't, I'm wetting the baby's head. Who's with me?*

Theo chuckled; Jenson was determined to enjoy his final baby-free pint if it killed him. As far as his mate was concerned, it might be the last time Jenson would be able to sink more than a couple of drinks, because if the baby woke Bella up (which she would), then Bella would most assuredly wake Jenson up. And Jenson had already moaned that it would possibly be years before Bella trusted anyone to babysit overnight, so even if he did manage a night out on the town, he'd be facing an early morning with a tiny child in the house. Hangovers and kids weren't a good combination. But tonight Bella and Baby would still be in hospital (jaundice, which meant the baby had to be placed under some kind of light – Jenson's details were vague), so his mate fully intended to enjoy every second of his unexpected freedom.

Dave: *I'd better check with Sadie, but if she's OK with it then count me in.*

Henry: *Can we go to the Student Union bar?*

Theo: *Aren't we a bit old?*

Henry: *I'm sure they'd let us in.*

Jenson: *Theo won't like it – they don't serve artisan beers there.*

Dave: *I like gin.*

Jenson: *That's because you're a big girl's blouse.*

Theo: *You can't say things like that, it's not PC.*

Jenson: *FFS, we're getting old. Gin, fancy beers and now we can't call our mates names because it's not PC. The rest of us have got an excuse for getting old because of our other halves, what's yours, Theo?*

Theo: *I've always been the grown up one out of you bunch of adolescents.*

Dave: *There's nothing wrong with liking gin. It's trendy.*

Archie: *The nearest you came to trendy was that daft haircut you had back in the second year at uni. Remember? I think I've got a photo somewhere.*

Dave: *Sod off, Archie. At least my hair grew back, you can't say the same for your face.*

Archie: *I can't help it if the girls used to fall all over me. You're just jealous.*

Henry: *They used to fall at your feet because you had bad breath, man.*

Archie: *That's harsh!*

Jenson: *Oi! About tonight? Who's coming out for a pint?'*

Theo: *What time and where?*

Jenson: *Theo, the lucky sod, doesn't have to check with his missus if he's allowed out to play.*

Dave: *That's because he doesn't have one.*

Archie: *True. Lucky sod.*

Theo: *Actually, I do.*

Henry: *Do what? Have to ask your mum?* This was followed by several rolling on the floor laughing emojis.

Theo: *I do have a other half.* He was grinning as he typed it, almost bursting with the news, and he waited for the insults to start.

Nothing. Not a peep out of any of them..He checked his phone; it appeared to be working fine. Maybe he'd lost connection for a second?

Jenson: *For real?*

Finally, someone had responded. He'd been beginning to think the shock might have struck them all dead.

Theo: **Yep**. Smiley face times five.

Archie: **How long? I mean, you didn't just meet her in a pub last night, swap phone numbers, and now you think you're in a deep and meaningful relationship?**

Theo: **A couple of weeks.**

Jenson: **You kept that quiet.**

Henry: **Too quiet. He's making it up.**

Theo: **No, I'm not!**

Jenson: **Prove it.**

Theo thought for a moment, then posted several photos.

Jenson: **Pretty, but she could be anyone.**

Theo: **Her name is Josie.**

Dave: **Have you got any of the two of you together? Bet he hasn't, cause he's making it up.**

Henry: **Aw, Theo's got an imaginary friend.**

Theo did have one. It wasn't the most flattering photo of him, but he knew if he didn't post it on the chat, his mates would continue to take the mickey. Josie had taken it the other day when they were out with the dogs, and they had their heads together, Josie trying to kiss him while staring into the camera and trying to hold her phone at the same time.

Jenson: **Bloody hell, mate. Well done – she's a stunner.**

Archie: *Welcome to the club. You're now an official member.*

For Theo, sharing the news with his friends made it feel even more real. He was now one half of a couple, and he was loving every minute of it. He knew his mates did, too. The banter was part of who they were and how the group interacted, but he knew for a fact that Jenson worshipped the ground Bella walked on.

Henry: *Is she a teacher?*

Theo: *Canine care professional.* That should flummox then for a second.

Archie: *???*

Theo: *Dog walker/dog sitter.*

Jenson: *Bloody hell, mate, I told you that dog was a babe magnet! I gotta get me one of them!*

Yeah, right; as if...

Theo, Jenson and Henry arranged to meet in a pub in town later on that evening, with Dave showing up if and when his missus said he could, and Theo found he was looking forward to a night out. Poppy had been on three decent walks today and he'd have a good play session with her before he left, so she should settle down quickly enough, and he wouldn't be back late. It would do her good to be left on her own for a few hours, because as lovely as she was, she couldn't be with him all the time. There were occasions, like tonight, when he'd have to leave her at home.

But, as much as he was anticipating an enjoyable drink with his friends, there was a part of him (quite a large part) that wished he was spending it with his girlfriend and his dog instead.

CHAPTER 28

The bar was as busy and as noisy as Theo remembered it being. He hadn't had a drink in this particular pub for years, but it hadn't changed a bit. It used to be one of their old stomping grounds, when they'd been young, free and skint. The beer had been cheap, the food had been plentiful and it hadn't been too far to stagger home at the end of the evening.

Theo looked around curiously. It certainly was a blast from the past, and he smiled at some of the memories the place evoked. Would he want to live those years over again? Not a chance. He was perfectly happy with his life the way it was, thank you, and he didn't have the slightest wish to revisit his youth.

Jenson clearly did, because he was sitting at a table with three empty pint glasses lined up in front of him, and was busy downing a fourth. He was on his own and Theo guessed he had drunk those pints all by himself.

'You've started without us,' Theo said, resting his hand on the back of a chair. 'Unless everyone else has disappeared off to the gents?'

'Right first time,' Jenson said, wiping froth from his mouth with the back of his hand.

'You look knackered, fella,' Theo pointed out, after he returned from the bar with a couple of pints. He handed one to Jenson and he took a deep swallow out of the other one.

'Thirty-six hours she was in labour, and I had to be awake for every damned one of them. Why, I ask you? Why?'

'Uh… moral support?'

'Huh! It was more like she wanted someone to gripe at. Thirty-six hours.'

'Don't you think you should go easy on the alcohol? You're going to pass out at this rate.'

'Good. That's what I'm aiming for.' Jenson stared at him with bleary red-rimmed eyes. 'Christ, what have I done?' he murmured, and those eyes filled with unshed tears.

Theo glanced away, uncomfortably. Where the hell were Dave and Henry? He wasn't cut out for comforting grown men when they were upset. And what was he supposed to say to Jenson, who was obviously regretting having the baby? Theo didn't have any experience with this kind of thing.

'It'll be all right, mate,' he said, awkwardly patting Jenson on the shoulder. 'It's bound to be a shock. I mean, you knew it was going to happen, but I don't suppose anything can prepare you for when the baby is actually here.'

Jenson didn't say anything; he simply stared morosely into his half-empty glass.

'Oh, what do I know?' Theo sighed. 'I haven't exactly been there and done that, have I? You'd be better off speaking to Dave. He's done this sort of thing twice. He'll set your mind at rest. I'm sure once Bella and the baby are home you'll settle into a routine and…' He trailed off. He didn't know what he was talking about, and he couldn't imagine being in Jenson's position of becoming a father and not being sure how to deal with it.

'She's… man, she's….' Jenson said, struggling for the words.

Theo winced. Where the hell was Dave? Dave would know what to say. Even Henry would do at a push, because at least he'd be moral support. Theo felt totally out of his depth.

'She's what?' he asked, then an awful thought occurred to him. 'The baby is all right, isn't she?'

'She's beautiful. When Jenson looked at Theo, he saw that his friend's expression was one of total and utter love. 'I can't believe I made her.'

'Er, I think you had a bit of help.'

'She's got my eyes. And when she looks at you, she sees right into your soul.'

Crikey, how many more drinks had Jenson had before he arrived, he wondered. The guy was three sheets to the wind. Happily drunk, but drunk all the same, and Theo couldn't help smiling at his friend.

'Want to see a photo?' Jenson asked, and he nodded.

Jenson handed him his phone and Theo scrolled through image after image of a tiny baby – on her own in a cot, being held by Bella, being held by Jenson, being held by Jenson's mum, being held by a woman who Theo assumed was Bella's mum, suckling from Bella's— Oh, no, he didn't want to see that. Bella probably wouldn't want him to see that, either. Hastily, he handed the phone back.

'Got any photos?' Dave asked from over his shoulder, and Theo breathed a sigh of relief. Only to immediately tense again when Jenson gave Dave the phone.

'Don't look at the ones where Bella's feeding the baby,' he warned.

'It's OK, Sadie breastfed both of ours. She is still feeding the youngest herself. I've seen it all before,' Dave said, airily.

'You haven't seen Bella's, mate, believe me. And Bella will kill you if she finds out you have.'

Dave's expression was suitably alarmed, and he swiftly handed the phone back. 'Another pint for you, Jenson?'

Jenson nodded, finishing the dregs in his glass and handing it to Dave for a refill.

'Do you want another?' Dave asked Theo.

He shook his head. 'I've hardly touched this one, thanks all the same.'

A group of women on a nearby table broke out into gales of laughter and Theo glanced over. One of them vaguely reminded him of Josie (only vaguely, and it was the dark hair that did it), and he wondered what she was doing now. He could picture her curled up in her favourite armchair, a book in her hand and Crumble wedged into the seat beside her. There'd hardly be sufficient room for them both, but neither human nor dog appeared to care. Until Crumble got too hot and slithered off the chair to lie on the cooler tiles in the kitchen, that is.

Then he wondered what Poppy was doing, and he resisted the temptation to get his phone out to check on her. She'd be fine. He'd not been gone long, only just over an hour. Surely he could manage eighty-one minutes without seeing she was OK for himself?

He lasted ten more minutes and when Henry finally

arrived, he used the excuse of going to the bar to get another round in, to fish out his phone and click on the camera app.

Poppy wasn't in her basket.

She was on her feet and staring up at the window, at full attention with her ears pricked.

Aww, bless her, she'd probably spotted a bird.

Hang on, though, she wasn't her normal waggy-tailed self, so maybe she'd seen something else? Her tail was low, not quite curled underneath her body, and her back was hunched slightly. Whatever it was, she didn't like it.

Theo wished he had a better angle, but all he could see was the very edge of the windowsill up in the top right-hand side of the screen. The old phone was angled to show as much of the floor as possible and especially Poppy's basket and the door to the garden, where she liked to sit on the little mat and watch the birdy goings-on outside.

She jerked, and Theo turned the volume up in time to hear her bark again.

He hadn't heard that particular noise come out of her little mouth before, and he was surprised at the depth and volume of the sound. Poppy wasn't going to be a yapper – the bark was deeper than he expected and whatever it was she was shouting, she meant every single woof of it.

Curious, he continued to watch as she turned slowly away from the window and angled herself towards the door. She'd stopped barking now and was listening intently, her head cocked.

Suddenly, she leapt backwards on stiff paws, barking frantically, and it took Theo a second to realise what had frightened her.

A shadow fell across the door, spreading onto the tiles and over Poppy herself, and Theo gasped when the figure of a man came into view. The bloke cautiously peered around the edge of the door and into the kitchen, before turning away to scan the garden.

Theo watched as he looked up at the bedroom windows, then across to his neighbours, then the fellow stared into the kitchen again.

Poppy was going berserk; she was patently scared, as her stiff-legged stance and loud barks testified, and she continued to back away from the door.

The man tapped on the glass, then took out his phone and pointed it at Poppy.

The git was photographing her.

He had to get home right now!

Enraged and more than a little worried, Theo shot out of the pub, one eye on the screen, one eye keeping a look out for a taxi.

'Come on, come on,' he growled, craning his head to see down the street.

A noise emanating from his phone caught his attention, and he glanced back at the screen to see the man rattling the door handle.

Thank God for mortice locks! The only way the bloke was going to get through the door was if he broke the glass, and that would take some doing. It would make a great deal of noise too; enough, Theo hoped, to alert his neighbours. Arnie played bowls on a Tuesday evening, but Felicity should be at home.

Oh, my God, he thought, frantically – what if the man did break his door and Felicity came out to investigate and—?

'Get away from there!' Theo yelled into his phone at the top of his voice. 'Get off my property before I call the police!'

He wasn't sure how loud the volume was at Poppy's end, but she certainly heard him as she almost leapt out of her skin at his frantic shout.

The man must have heard something too, because he narrowed his beady eyes and craned his neck to stare at the rear of the cottage, his eyes darting everywhere. Then he turned his attention to the door itself, until finally, seeing nothing untoward, the bloke examined the kitchen. But this time he wasn't looking at Poppy. He was looking directly at Theo's old mobile phone and he didn't look happy.

'I can see you!' Theo shouted at the top of his voice.

'I'm phoning the police right now.'

He wasn't sure whether he could make a phone call and view the camera app at the same time, and he was too terrified of what might happen if he stopped watching, but to his immense relief a taxi responded to his violent arm-waving and pulled over just as the intruder backed away from the kitchen door.

Theo leapt into the cab, gave the driver his address and asked him to please hurry. 'I've just seen someone on camera trying to break into my house. I think he's trying to steal my dog.'

'There's been a spate of dog thefts,' the driver said, catching Theo's eye. 'You say they're at your house right now?'

'They were there two seconds ago.'

'Hang on, I'll see what I can do.'

Theo waited with bated breath, hardly daring to blink as the taxi driver called the office and explained the situation, adding that the controller should call the police and asking if they had anyone in the vicinity of Theo's house.

'We have. I'll ask them to swing by and toot their horn. I don't want to put any of my drivers in danger, but the noise might be enough to scare the bugger off,' the controller said, and Theo stammered his heartfelt thanks.

He didn't care if there was any damage, but if the

man did get in and take Poppy, Theo didn't know what he'd do. An image of John Wick, gun in one hand and a knife in the other jumped into his head, and he gritted his teeth.

If he managed to get his hands on that bloke...

Theo found himself curling his hands into fists, and a surge of anger greater than he had ever experienced in his life before, swept through him. If anything happened to that poor defenceless little dog, he wouldn't be responsible for his actions.

'I'm outside the address now, but I can't see nothing,' a tinny voice came over the radio several minutes later and Theo wondered if he could dare to breathe again. 'Nah, whoever it was has scarpered.'

'Thank you, thank you,' he stuttered.

'Can't see no damage either, but there's a dirty big scuff mark on the back gate, so it looks like they climbed over that.'

'Please, tell the driver I owe him one. I owe all of you. Thank you, so much.' He slumped back in the seat, his heart thumping so hard, he thought it might leap out of his chest, and his hands were all clammy.

He felt sick with relief and consumed with worry over Poppy. His poor little girl must be totally traumatised, and his eyes swam with unexpected tears as he thought of what she must be going through.

'No worries, glad to help,' the taxi driver said, and

Theo nodded his gratitude, not trusting himself to speak.

The journey seemed to take an age, but it couldn't have been more than twenty minutes, and when the cab pulled up outside the cottage, he thrust double the amount of the fare showing on the clock at the driver, uttered garbled thanks and dashed inside the house.

It was deathly quiet. Normally he'd hear Poppy's claws on the tiles as she trotted to wait by the kitchen door in order to be in prime position to launch herself at him as soon as he opened it, but this evening the silence chilled him to the bone.

'Poppy?' His voice was hesitant and filled with dread as he turned the handle and slowly pushed the door to the kitchen open.

The pup was standing in the middle of the room, her tail and ears down, a worried expression on her little face, and it took her a moment to realise the person framed in the doorway was Theo.

When she did, she let out a whimper and scuttled towards him, low to the ground, her tail curled under her. Theo dropped to his knees as the dog leapt into his arms, the whimpers turning into yips and her body wriggling with excitement, which Theo translated as relief. This greeting felt different from all the others she had given him over the previous weeks; he couldn't explain it, but it felt to him that Poppy was incredibly thankful he was home. The fact that she was refusing to be put down (she liked to dance around his feet) and was burying her nose in his neck reinforced his opinion.

A knock on the door took him by surprise, and he warily clambered to his feet, the dog still in his arms, and he went to answer it.

Mindful that the man might have returned and was trying a different tactic (a grab and run tactic, maybe?) Theo looked through the living room window first. He didn't mind admitting that he was unnerved, and he wasn't looking forward to spending the night on his own when there was a prowler around.

It was the police.

'That was quick,' Theo said, inviting them in.

'We had a call from Appy Cabs to say you witnessed a break-in at your property?'

'Ah, yes, not a break-in as such, but a man was scoping the place out, and he took photos. He even tried the handle.' It sounded much less dramatic than it had been.

'And where were you at the time, sir?'

'Out with friends. I've got a new puppy,' he jerked his head at the dog nestled in his arms, 'and I wanted to check on her. She's not used to being left on her own. Do you want to sit down? And would you like a tea or coffee?'

'No, thanks.' The policeman's eyes were everywhere, darting around the room, taking everything in. 'CCTV, is it?'

'Not exactly. I use an old phone as a camera, and there's an app you can download.'

The man nodded. 'I know of it. It's useful. Can I see the footage?'

'What footage?'

'The app uses motion detection to record events, and stores them for thirty days. Can I see your phone?'

Theo had no idea the facility existed. Handing his mobile over, he shuffled the puppy into a more comfortable position and hoped he hadn't been doing anything embarrassing in his kitchen. Then he remembered kissing Josie soundly by the sink one day, and his cheeks grew warm.

'Take a look.' The copper angled the phone so the other police officer could see it.

'Well, well, well. He's out, is he?'

'Who is? Out from where?' Theo asked.

'This man is well known to us,' the policeman explained. 'He was sent down a couple of years ago for aggravated burglary. Can we take a look out the back?'

Theo showed them into the kitchen and opened the door leading out to the garden. The officers spent a few minutes examining the gate and the wall.

'Can you arrest him?' he wanted to know.

'He's not done anything illegal this evening, apart from trespassing, but we'd be lucky if we could get that to stick. We will have a word with him, though. Give him a warning that we're on to him.'

'You might want to ask him about Mrs Barnett's Sugarplum,' Theo suggested.

The two officers exchanged a look. 'Mrs Barnett's Sugarplum…?'

'Her dog. A Pomeranian. Very expensive. It was stolen from her garden a week or so ago.

The policemen exchanged another look, but this time it was filled with meaning not puzzlement.

'There has been a series of dog thefts, recently,' one of them said. 'Do you think he was after yours?'

'Most definitely. You saw him taking photos of her. She's not a pedigree, she's a hybrid, a mix of Cocker spaniel and poodle, but I think my parents gave a fair bit for her.'

'It's your parents' dog, is it? And is this their house?'

'She's my dog and it's my house. She was a gift.'

'I see. And you think the dog is valuable?'

'Yes.' She was extremely valuable to him, indeed.

'We'll look into it, sir, thank you.'

'What happens now?'

'I suggest you remain vigilant and if you have any further concerns, call us.'

'Right, OK, thanks.'

'We'll see ourselves out.'

Oh no, you won't, Theo thought, following closely behind the two men and locking the door as soon as they left. He was also going to keep his back door locked from now on, too. Gone were the days when he'd leave it open so Poppy could wander in and out at will. If she was in the garden, then he intended to be out there too. It was going to be a bit of a pain, but if that's what it took to keep his pup safe, then so be it.

Josie!

He needed to tell her what happened, and not because he wanted to hear the sound of her voice, either (although he did) – she needed to know about this because of Crumble.

He wasn't at all surprised when she insisted on coming straight round.

CHAPTER 29

Theo would have gone to Josie's house, but Poppy was happy cuddling up to him and she'd had enough upset for one day, so he didn't want to disturb her. And he was glad he didn't because the pup didn't want to be put down even to greet her beloved Crumble and Josie. Instead, she whimpered a little and wagged her tail from the safety of her master's embrace. Which made hugging a very worried and extremely concerned Josie rather difficult.

'Tell me again,' she demanded, and Theo recounted the story for the third (or was it the fourth?) time that evening.

'I can't believe it,' she kept saying. 'What a horrible thing to have happened.'

He noticed that she'd kept one hand on Crumble at all times since she'd stepped through his door, and he understood how she felt; he didn't want to let go of

Poppy either. Returning to work in just over a week was going to prove very difficult indeed, and he was dreading it.

'I'm going to get an alarm fitted,' he said, 'and some proper cameras, one on the front and one on the back of the house. I simply can't take a chance of this happening again.'

'Thank God you checked your camera when you did,' she said.

'I know. I hate to think what might have happened if I hadn't, and I'm so thankful it has sound on it. I'm sure my screaming down the phone scared the blighter off. Unfortunately, it scared Poppy, too.'

'She'll be fine,' Josie reassured him. 'I'm sure she knew that it wasn't her you were yelling at.'

'I'll have to thank Jenson when I see him next – if it wasn't for Bella wanting to spend a fortune on a baby monitor and Jenson finding a cheap alternative, I would never have known about the phone camera app.' He paused and slapped a palm to his forehead as he remembered something, making the already nervous pup jump.

'Sorry, Poppy, I didn't mean to scare you,' he told her, kissing the top of her head. He pulled a face as he said to Josie, 'I owe the guys an explanation. I was supposed to be getting the drinks in and I just disappeared without telling them where I was going.'

When he looked at his phone again, he saw he had lots of messages. They'd started off in a teasing vein but as the time went on they gradually became more concerned. He checked the time, surprised to see that only an hour and a half had passed since he'd dashed out of the pub. They'd still be there, so he decided to call Henry, on the premise that Jenson would probably be too drunk to locate his phone, never mind being sober enough to answer it.

Henry picked up on the third ring, and once Theo had explained what happened, was totally sympathetic.

'I'll come out for a drink another time,' Theo promised, when he heard Jenson in the background demanding to know whether Theo was going to return to the pub. 'I've got Josie here and Poppy would be perfectly safe with her, but I don't want to leave her.'

'Which "her" are you referring to?' Henry asked. 'The girlfriend or the dog? Bloomin' heck, the lengths some people will go to not to miss seeing their other half for a night.'

Theo smiled. They were back to taking the mickey out of him, so he could tell they thought he was OK. He ended the call and turned his attention back to Josie. 'They want to meet you,' he said, 'because they think I'm making you up.'

'When and where?' she responded, without hesitation.

'Soon; I want to keep you all to myself for a while. Besides, I don't think you're ready for that lot, yet. They might put you off me.'

Josie scooted across the sofa and cuddled up next to him, Poppy between them. 'Nothing can put me off you.'

'Not even when you know I have watched Mama Mia twice?'

She nuzzled into him. Poppy, with a disgusted look, wriggled free and jumped onto the floor.

'I love Mama Mia,' Josie murmured, taking his earlobe between her teeth and nibbling gently.

Theo let out a groan. 'You'd better stop doing that, or I won't be responsible for my actions.

'Oh goody, I was hoping it would have that effect on you.'

She carried on nibbling until he was unable to stand it anymore, and he drew her into his arms and teased her mouth with his lips.

Josie let out a slow sigh, her breath mingling with his, and desire coursed through him.

His last coherent thought before her kisses swept him away was that he loved this woman more than life itself.

CHAPTER 30

This first day of the new academic year had come around all too quickly. He wasn't ready for it and he wasn't entirely certain it was ready for him, even though it was a training day and there were no pupils as yet. His colleagues weren't ready either, that much was obvious. But something was different this year…

He'd changed, he knew he had, and that change was noticeable. His face hadn't changed and neither had the rest of him, not in a physical sense, because he'd still looked the same in his bathroom mirror when he'd shaved last night as he had on any other workday. But something must have alerted his fellow staff members to the difference because several of them had done a double-take when they'd seen him.

'Christ, where have you been on holiday?' Mr Donald cried. 'I need to pay it a visit.'

'I've not been anywhere,' Theo replied. 'I stayed

home all summer.'

'Are you on antidepressants? Is that it?'

'Excuse me?'

'You don't look as miserable as you usually do. Mind you, I've been off for a bit as you know, so I might have missed something. Have you got another job? Is that why you look so damned happy, because you're escaping from this place?'

'It's not that bad,' Theo objected.

To which Mr Donald replied in a loud whisper because the head teacher had arrived in the hall to go through the exam results with the staff, '10.3. Remember them?'

'They'll be 11.3 now, and I've got a feeling they'll settle down and pull their fingers out. Year 11s normally do when they realise this is their final year.'

Mr Donald harrumphed and shrugged his shoulders.

Maybe the drama teacher had a point and 10.3 – now 11.3 – would be just as horrendous as they'd been last year, but he hoped that one of them at least would come back to school after the summer holidays with an improved attitude and a better work ethic.

He nodded and smiled at several people, all of whom looked as resigned as he felt, but it was true that he wasn't as despondent as he usually was at the start of term. In fact, he felt quite chirpy, although he was missing Josie and Poppy terribly.

At least he knew the pup was in good hands, as he'd dropped her off at Josie's house before he went to work – it was a great excuse to have breakfast with his girlfriend, too – and he'd pick the pup up in the evening and have yet another excuse to eat dinner together. Actually, neither he nor Josie needed an excuse, as they'd hardly been out of each other's sight since the night of the attempted dog snatch, and Josie was spending more and more time at the cottage than she was in her own house. She appeared to be perfectly happy with the situation, and Theo was over the moon about it. The two dogs missed each other when they were apart too, and Theo was thankful that the pooches got on so brilliantly.

His phone pinged and he took a sneaky peep, while pretending to listen to Mr Fitzpatrick as he wittered on about percentage ratios compared to similar schools in the county and across England. Then he smiled as he realised he was behaving as badly as the kids he taught when they got their phones out in class hoping he wouldn't notice that they were staring intently at their laps – just as he was doing,

His smile grew wider as he saw the photo Josie had sent him. The dogs were out on their walk with another two of Josie's charges for the day, and she'd taken them to a field where she could let all the hounds off the lead and allow them to scamper about to their heart's content without fear of them escaping.

The rest of the day followed a similar pattern as other years, as the teaching staff returned to their various departments for further dissection of the results and to plan for the year ahead. And periodically, Josie sent him photos, or the occasional text, or an emoji kiss.

He couldn't wait to get home to see them both, and Crumble too, of course, because he'd grown rather fond of the batty spaniel and his older brother protectiveness of Poppy. The four of them worked well together, they made a good team, and he was seriously considering asking Josie an important question. Maybe not tonight, but when the time was right he intended to ask her to move in with him. It seemed silly for them to run two separate households when Josie was at his place most of the time. And moving in with him didn't mean she'd have to give up her independence – she could rent her house out, enough to cover her mortgage and provide a small additional income. He'd thought about it seriously, and looked at the figures, so all that was needed now was for him to ask her and for her to say yes.

To his surprise, the police were waiting for him when he arrived home later that day, having collected Josie and the dogs on the way.

As he parked his car, Theo studied their faces for any hint of whether they were the bearers of good news or bad, but it wasn't until he'd invited them in and Josie had popped the kettle on that they told him why they were there. It was the same pair who'd attended the scene on that night (he was pleased he knew some of the terminology, which was a result of Josie's fascination with watching reality police shows on TV) and he was keen to hear what they had to say.

'We've arrested the man who attempted to gain access to your house,' one of the officers said. 'In conjunction with several others who have been targeting dogs and stealing them to order.

'A bit like Gone in Sixty Seconds, except with dogs not cars,' Theo exclaimed.

'Er… quite. They've been charged with numerous offences and all of them have been convicted previously, so they'll probably receive custodial sentences.'

'How about Sugarplum?' Josie wanted to know. 'Have you found her?'

The men looked at one another in bafflement, so Theo reminded them. 'A Pomeranian owned by Mrs Barnett on Oswestry Drive.'

'Ah yes, Unfortunately, not yet. But we are hopeful and a couple of those arrested are currently helping us with our enquires. Actually helping,' he added, seeing the scepticism on Theo's face. 'So I'm sure it's only a matter of time.'

'Thank you for letting us know. We can sleep a bit easier knowing you've caught the people responsible.' Theo held out a hand and they shook it.

'I see you've heightened your security,' the second officer said. 'Is there CCTV out the back as well?'

'Of course, I'm not taking any chances with the ones I love,' Theo said. 'Whether they be human or canine.'

'Very wise.'

After they'd gone, he held his arms out to Josie and she stepped into them. 'That's a weight off my mind,' he said into her hair. 'But I'm glad we've got the alarm fitted and the camera system.'

'We? I haven't got an alarm on my house. Do you think I should?'

'Yeah… er… about that. I wasn't going to say anything yet, maybe leave it a while, but I miss you terribly when you're not here, and I know you have your own place, and you like your independence, but I've been thinking and—' He paused to take a much-needed breath and found he couldn't go on.

'And…?' she prompted, leaning back slightly so she could look him in the eye.

And… I wondered if you'd like to move in. Here. With me. You and Crumble. The two of you together, in this house, with me.' He ground to a halt.

Josie's eyes were wide and her mouth was open slightly. 'I… um… didn't expect that,' she said.

'I'm not suggesting you give up your own house, or anything, but you could move in here for a couple of weeks, or months, and see how it goes, and if you like it, I mean if we get on and it's working then you could rent yours out and you would still have your own place, because I'd hate for you to feel trapped. It's just that I miss you so much when you're not here, and I know we can't be together all the time – I mean, I have to work – but I'd like to spend the time when I'm not in work with you. Not all of it, obviously, because you have to have some "me" time, but—' He stopped abruptly, aware he was babbling and speaking too fast, and not making a great deal of sense. What he *was* doing was making a total arse of himself.

Josie was silent and Theo was convinced he'd blown it. He knew he should have waited; seven weeks between first meeting and asking someone to move in was far too soon. No wonder she was going to say no. He'd say no if he was in her shoes. She hardly knew him – she'd not met his friends yet or his parents. Oh, God, his *mum*. Josie hadn't even met his mum, and here he was asking her to live with him.

'Yes, I'd like that,' she replied slowly. 'I miss you too, and I'm aware that it hasn't been long, but I don't think there's a time limit on love, is there?'

Mutely he shook his head, his heart soaring. She'd said yes. Yes!

'I just want to ask one thing, in the interest of honesty and openness,' she said.

'Okaaay…?'

'It's not just because you want a full-time carer for Poppy is it?'

'No! Of course it—!' He saw the smile on her face and the teasing light in her eyes, and stopped protesting, kissing her soundly before she could tease him anymore.

As he gave himself to her soft lips, he knew he'd given all of himself to her, body and soul, and that meeting Josie was the best thing that had ever happened to him.

Poppy's nose nudged his leg, reminding him that he'd never have found Josie if it hadn't been for the love of a small, cute dog and he knew she'd forever have his gratitude as well as his heart.

'There is one thing,' he said, pulling away from Josie for a second. 'You need to know that someone else is in my heart, and she's pretty and cute and she loves me unconditionally. Can you accept that? Because if you can't, there's no future for us.'

Josie glanced at Poppy, then at Crumble. 'I wouldn't have it any other way,' she declared. 'Now stop talking and kiss me.'

Theo did as he was told.

CHAPTER 31

Theo didn't swear very often, but a few choice words almost slipped out of his mouth a couple of days later when he had 11.3 for their first maths lesson of the new academic year, because none other than Ron Elder was parked in a seat towards the back of the class. Tim Hogan and Cory Denham were flanking him, like a couple of teenage bodyguards.

He closed his mouth with a snap before his shock became verbal.

'Gentlemen,' he said, mildly. 'Nice to see you.'

He got a couple of eye rolls and a grunt in return, but at least they were there and they seemed to be working, he noticed, towards the end of the lesson, Ronnie especially. He'd kept a close eye on the three of them since it was those and another couple of boys who were the ringleaders when it came to disruptive behaviour and defiance of the rules and regulations, but there'd hardly been a peep out of them all lesson. Theo was beginning to wonder what the catch was. Were they setting him up for a fall? Lulling him into a false sense of security?

It wouldn't surprise him.

A minute or so before the bell was due to sound, Theo was making packing away noises, when Ronnie said, 'How's your dog, sir?'

Theo blinked, surprised that Ronni remembered he had a dog. 'She's great, thanks Growing fast. She's almost five months.'

One of the girls said, 'What have you got? I can imagine you with one of them little terrier things, you know, the ones what has bows in their hair.'

The rest of the class sniggered, and Lisa Jeffries smirked, enjoying her brief moment in the limelight.

'Not really,' he replied, bringing up his screensaver and flashing it onto the interactive whiteboard for everyone to see.

It was a photo of Poppy not long after he'd first been given her, and she was shy and nervous and staring into the lens with big eyes. It was one of the cutest he had of her, although every image was cute. She just looked especially sweet in this one.

There was a chorus of 'ahhs' and 'oohs' from the class, accompanied by squeals from the girls and a variety of comments along the lines of how cute she was, followed by a barrage of questions about her; all of which he tried to answer.

'I want to work with dogs when I leave school,' one of the quieter girls said with a hopeful look on her face, which was soon wiped off when she found herself on the receiving end of a whole load of derision from the others.

'What, like taking your boyfriend's Alsatian round the block? He's not gonna pay you for that,' Emma Pierson chortled.

'Well, she ain't got the smarts to be a vet!' Simone Simons joined in.

'There are other jobs working with animals,' Theo pointed out, signalling for the class to pipe down. 'Animal behaviourist, dog training, police dog handler…' The last one was met with hisses and boos.

'My mum's friend is a dog groomer,' someone said.

'And remember Milly Preston who used to be head girl when we were in the first year? She's a veterinary nurse now.'

Theo studied their faces, and realised there was one thing that most of those kids didn't have – belief in themselves.

'Let me tell you a story,' he said, glancing at the clock.' We've got time and it'll only take a minute.' He ignored the groans. 'I know a lady, an intelligent lady with a degree, who decided what she truly wanted to do was to work with dogs. She didn't want to be a vet, and neither did she want to be a nurse. What she wanted to do was to look after dogs all day long. So that's what she did – it's what she still does. She walks other people's dogs, looks after them in their own homes sometimes, and even has them staying with her if their owners want to go on holiday. Now, it might not be the best-paid job in the world and it might not be the most prestigious, but do you know what? She's one of the happiest people I know, and all because she loves her job. So don't let anyone tell you what career path is right for you. Do something that makes you happy, and only you know what that is.'

'Does that mean I don't have to come to school?'

'No, Saul, it does not mean you don't have to come to school. I realise that for most of you, school isn't your favourite place, but use it as a tool to get the qualifications you need to do a job that makes you smile every day, or one that you're passionate about.' A loud buzzer interrupted him. 'And, there's the bell. Off you go, and don't forget to have a go at that past paper I gave you at the start of the lesson for homework…' He found he was shouting this last to an empty classroom.

Almost empty.

One pupil had stayed behind, hanging around at the back of the class and Theo raised his eyebrows.

'Ronnie? Can I help you with something?'

'My mum's boyfriend, her latest one, has been nicked.'

'He has? Oh…' What was he supposed to say to that? Commiserations?

'Do you know what for?' Ronnie continued.

Theo shrugged. 'No idea.' Should he have?

'Pinching dogs.'

Ah. He grimaced. Quickly adding up two and two and getting to the nice round figure of four, Theo immediately understood what Ronnie was getting at. And maybe who Ronnie's mum's boyfriend was. Was this why Ronnie had turned up in school today, to confront him? And was Ronnie the reason this man had known about Poppy?

Abruptly Theo was thankful that the boy was still at the rear of the classroom and the door was near the front. He didn't think Ronnie was the type to become aggressive, but you never could tell, and the lad had skipped so many lessons that Theo didn't feel he knew him well enough to anticipate what he might do.

'Jabba, that's Mum's boyfriend – ex boyfriend, now – went round to yours, didn't he?' Ronnie said rather than asked, because he quite clearly knew the answer to his own question.

'Yes, he did.'

'And you called the cops on him, didn't you?'

'Yes.' Theo lifted his chin. He'd done nothing wrong; he was the victim in all this, and he didn't see why he should deny it. It was about time that kids learnt that actions had consequences.

Ronnie moved towards him, slowly. Theo debated backing away.

'Sorry, sir. It was my fault, him knowing about your dog.'

'You told him?'

'Not him; I was telling my mum and sister about it. *He* was there, Jabba. I didn't know he was pinching dogs, did I? Not then. Cause if I had, I wouldn't have said nuffink.'

'I see.' Theo wasn't entirely sure he did see, but he was at a loss for anything else to say.

'That's why I'm in school.'

'I don't follow.'

'Cause he's been nicked.' Ronnie grinned, the smile spreading across his face and lighting it up like the sun coming out from behind a cloud. 'My mum's well shot of him.'

'Oh, so you're not upset that he's been arrested then?'

'Fu— shit, no! I'm well chuffed.' The sun went back in for a moment as Ronnie's face clouded over. 'He used to hit her.'

'Ronnie... I'm so sorry. Maybe if you'd have come

to me, I could have—'

'Pasted him? Not likely. He'd have had you for breakfast.'

'I was going to say, contacted social services or…' Theo trailed off, seeing Ronnie's expression.

'No. Not them. Never the socials.'

'Did he ever hit you?'

Ronnie looked away and bit his lip. Then his gaze returned to Theo, defiant and challenging him to say he was lying. 'Nah, he wouldn't have dared.'

It's a good job Jabba was in custody then, wasn't it, Theo thought, because he would have had to have told one of the school management team that Ronnie was in danger at home.

'Glad to have you back, Ronnie,' was all he said. 'Are you intending to stay?'

'That depends, don't it?'

'On what?'

'How good a teacher you are. Easily bored, me.'

'You cheeky… Go on, scoot, otherwise you'll be late for your next lesson.'

'Oh, and there's summat else.'

'What?'

'I know where that woman's dog is, the old biddy.'

'Mrs Barnett?'

'Yeah, her.'

'Where?'

'Back in her garden.'

'How—?

'You don't want to know.'

Theo thought that was very probably true...

Ronnie strolled nonchalantly out of the classroom, and Theo was left hoping that he would see considerably more of Ronnie Elder in his lessons.

Josie was astounded when he told her about it later, as they snuggled up on the sofa with the two dogs at their feet.

'Do you think he'll attend school more often now?' she asked.

'I'd like to think so. Do you know, I wasn't sure I wanted to continue teaching when school broke up for the summer, but now I realise it's what I want to carry on doing. When you get kids like Ronnie and Tim, and you see them starting to turn their attitudes around, then it makes it all worthwhile.'

He paused, thinking, his fingers winding absently through her hair. 'It's certainly been a more eventful summer than I thought it was going to be,' he mused. 'I think this summer is the best one I can ever remember. Not only have I fallen in love with a dog, I've also fallen back in love with my job. But more importantly, I've fallen in love with the most wonderful woman in the world.'

EPILOGUE

'Happy birthday to you, happy birthday to you,' Theo and Josie warbled. 'Happy birthday, dear Poppy, happy birthday to you.' He leaned closer so the patiently waiting dogs could sniff the home-made cake.

Two noses twitched and two tails wagged furiously. They knew they had a treat coming, and they sat perfectly still while Theo cut the cake and popped a slice into their respective bowls.

'I can't believe she's one already,' Theo said. 'Where has the past year gone? It seems like only yesterday I was watching my daft parents drive off leaving me with a tiny bundle and no clue what to do with it.'

'And now here you are, baking birthday cakes for dogs.' Josie stretched up to give him a kiss. 'Poppy isn't the only one who's getting a cake today,' she added.

He frowned, pretty sure it wasn't his birthday

because that had been back in March, and it wasn't the anniversary of him and Josie getting together, because that was August; he'd booked a surprise week away in a cottage in North Wales for that. The dogs would be coming too, naturally, and he was looking forward to exploring new places with them.

'Why?' he asked cautiously, hoping he hadn't missed something important.

'Because we haven't celebrated your promotion yet.'

'I thought we did that already.' He sent her a suggestive smile and she grinned wickedly back at him.

'That's not what I meant.'

'Do I get to celebrate twice?'

'Yes, but not in the way you mean.'

'Aww, spoilsport…'

'Dinner, wine, cake…?'

He sighed dramatically and rolled his eyes. 'If you insist. Although the cake is a bit over the top.'

'Blame your mum.'

'She's baked me a cake?'

'She's proud of you – we all are. It's not every day you get promoted to head of the maths department. So, we're going out to dinner tonight and she's going to present you with a cake at the end. You will appear surprised and delighted, else you won't get any dessert.'

Theo was puzzled. 'I thought the cake was dessert?'

'I'm talking about later, when we're on our own. 'She waggled her eyebrows at him and he let out a laugh. 'I know how much you hate surprises,' she continued, 'especially the ones your mum springs on you, so I thought I'd warn you. Although... I do have another surprise...'

She appeared uncertain, and he wondered what it could be. Not another dog, he hoped. He loved Poppy and Crumble to bits, and he couldn't imagine life without them, but he didn't want to go through the housetraining and teething stages again, not when these two were so well behaved.

'I'm... er... pregnant,' she blurted.

Theo froze. Then his heart began to thud, and he was filled with such intense joy he thought he was going to burst.

Trying to keep a blank expression on his face, he nodded slowly, and said, 'That's it, then. There's only one thing to be done.'

Josie's eyes were huge and she swallowed nervously. 'What?' she whispered, her voice catching.

Theo couldn't keep his elation in check any longer. 'We're going to have to get married,' he declared, smiling so widely he thought his face might crack.

'We are?'

He nodded. 'Wait there. I was going to do this in the summer, when we went— Never mind! I'll do it now.'

'Do what?' she called after him, as he dashed upstairs to retrieve a little box from where he'd hidden it in the bag he used for school.

'This!' he cried, flinging himself down the steps two at a time, careering down the hall and almost falling into the kitchen.

The dogs looked expectantly at him, as though they knew what he was about to do.

Skidding to a halt, he dropped to one knee, wincing slightly as the other collided with the tiled floor, and whipped the box out, opened it and held it up to her.

'Josie Wilde, will you do me the honour of marrying me?'

The confusion in her face was slowly replaced with shock, then delight.

'Yes, oh yes! I will. I do! I mean—' she cried.

He didn't give her a chance to tell him what she meant, because he leapt to his feet, flung his arms around her and silenced her with a long, blissful kiss.

And as he held her, he knew he'd hold her forever in his heart and his soul – along with the owners of two cold noses who were nudging their way in between them, to demand their fair share of the love and attention.

Because without them, and his darling Poppy in particular, Theo would never have found the woman he intended to spend the rest of his life with.

Doggy Birthday Cake Recipe

It's probably best not to feed your pup human sponge cake, but you can make your own doggy version which will be far healthier for your pooch, and you won't run the risk of upsetting his or her tummy. As a general rule, dogs love apples, and carrots are usually a firm favourite, too.

> 225g lean minced beef
> 75g rolled oats
> 75g peas and grated carrot
> 75g pureed apple
> 1 egg

Mix all the ingredients together and put in a baking tin. Bake at 180 centigrade for at least 45 minutes. Make sure the meat is thoroughly cooked by inserting a skewer into the centre and if it comes out clean, then the cake is done.

For the "frosting", use mashed potato or low fat creamed cheese, and decorate your cake with doggy chocs, bone-shaped biscuits, pieces of carrot or apple – in fact, you could probably use most of the dog-safe treats you usually give your pooch.

It might sound a revolting mix of random stuff, but your fur baby will love it!

More from Liz Davies

We hope you enjoyed reading The Summer of Falling in Love. If you did, please leave a review.

If you'd like to gift a copy, this book is also available in paperback.

Acknowledgements

A book doesn't come into being on its own. It usually takes a whole horde of people working behind the scenes, from the author, to the editor, to the proofreaders, the cover designer... Which means I have several people to thank.

Probably the first is my long-suffering hubby, who puts up with me hiding behind my laptop screen for hours on end. I also need to thank him for the idea for this book. When he realised the amount of attention he was receiving from ladies when he was out with our extremely cute puppy, he did suggest that having a puppy was better than Tinder. Not that he'd ever signed up to Tinder – or is that the start of another book!

Catherine Mills deserves a huge mention for putting up with my incessant chatter about writing without her eyes glazing over. She also edits my stories and she's so lovely with her advice and criticism. I don't know what I'd do without her.

And of course, you, my readers, need to be thanked. Without you, I wouldn't still be writing!

ABOUT THE AUTHOR

Liz Davies writes feel-good, light-hearted stories with a hefty dose of romance, a smattering of humour, and a great deal of love.

She's married to her best friend, has one grown-up daughter, and when she isn't scribbling away in the notepad she carries with her everywhere (just in case inspiration strikes), you'll find her searching for that perfect pair of shoes. She loves to cook but isn't very good at it, and loves to eat - she's much better at that! Liz also enjoys walking (preferably on the flat), cycling (also on the flat), and lots of sitting around in the garden on warm, sunny days.

She currently lives with her family in Wales, but would ideally love to buy a camper van and travel the world in it.

Social Media Links:
Twitter https://twitter.com/lizdaviesauthor
Facebook: fb.me/LizDaviesAuthor1